Wintersoft's CEO is on a husband hunt
for his daughter. Trouble is Emily has uncovered
his scheme. But can she marry off the eligible
executives before Dad sets his crazy plan in motion?

* * *

"You have a miracle in there."

"Two of them," Ariana responded.

Grant moved a hand to either side of her belly and
drew her to him. The babies moved beneath his touch.

They stood there, connected in a most elemental way,
and Grant's urge to share in her babies shifted and
changed. He had the most frightening need to pull her
closer, to lay his mouth over hers, to feel her heartbeat
against his.

Their glances connected. She knew he wanted to kiss
her and she wanted it, too.

Ariana Fitzpatrick, pregnant or not, was exquisite.
A dark and delicate beauty who caused him to feel
things he didn't want to feel and to think things he
had no business thinking.

With the great discipline he'd cultivated over the
years, he removed his hands and stepped away.

Dear Reader,

October is bringing big changes in the Silhouette and Harlequin worlds. To strengthen the terrific lineup of stories we offer, Silhouette Romance will be moving to four fabulous titles each month.

Don't miss the newest story in this six-book series— MARRYING THE BOSS'S DAUGHTER. In this second title, *Her Pregnant Agenda* (#1690) by Linda Goodnight, Emily Winters is up to her old matchmaking tricks. This time she has a bachelor lawyer and his alluring secretary—a single mom-to-be—on her matrimonial short list.

Valerie Parv launches her newest three-book miniseries, THE CARRAMER TRUST, with *The Viscount & the Virgin* (#1691). In it, an arrogant royal learns a thing or two about love from his secret son's sassy aunt. This is the third continuation of Parv's beloved Carramer saga.

An ornery M.D. is in danger of losing his heart to a sweet young nurse, in *The Most Eligible Doctor* (#1692) by reader favorite Karen Rose Smith. And is it possible to love a two-in-one cowboy? Meet the feisty teacher who does, in Doris Rangel's magical *Marlie's Mystery Man* (#1693), our latest SOULMATES title.

I encourage you to sample all four of these heartwarming romantic titles from Silhouette Romance this month.

Enjoy!

Mavis C. Allen
Associate Senior Editor, Silhouette Romance

Please address questions and book requests to:
Silhouette Reader Service
U.S.: 3010 Walden Ave., P.O. Box 1325, Buffalo, NY 14269
Canadian: P.O. Box 609, Fort Erie, Ont. L2A 5X3

Her Pregnant Agenda

LINDA GOODNIGHT

SILHOUETTE *Romance*®

Published by Silhouette Books

America's Publisher of Contemporary Romance

Special thanks and acknowledgment are given to
Linda Goodnight for her contribution to
the MARRYING THE BOSS'S DAUGHTER series.

For Gayle Warrington, who encouraged me from the beginning
and still awaits every book with enthusiasm and excitement.
Friends like you are hard to find.

 SILHOUETTE BOOKS

ISBN 0-373-19690-3

HER PREGNANT AGENDA

Copyright © 2003 by Harlequin Books S.A.

This edition published by arrangement with Harlequin Books S.A.

Visit Silhouette at www.eHarlequin.com

Printed in U.S.A.

Books by Linda Goodnight

Silhouette Romance

For Her Child... #1569
Married in a Month #1682
Her Pregnant Agenda #1690

LINDA GOODNIGHT

A romantic at heart, Linda Goodnight believes in the traditional values of family and home. Writing books enables her to share her certainty that, with faith and perseverance, love can last forever and happy endings really are possible.

A native of Oklahoma, Linda lives in the country with her husband, Gene, and Mugsy, an adorably obnoxious rat terrier. She and Gene have a blended family of six grown children. An elementary school teacher, she is also a licensed nurse. When time permits, Linda loves to read, watch football and rodeo and indulge in chocolate. She also enjoys taking long, calorie-burning walks in the nearby woods. Readers can write to her at linda@lindagoodnight.com.

FROM THE DESK OF EMILY WINTERS

Five
~~Six~~ Bachelor Executives To Go

Bachelor #1: Love, Your Secret Admirer
Matthew Burke—Hmm...his sweet ~~assistant clearly~~ has googly eyes for her workaholic ~~boss~~. ~~Maybe I can make some office magic happen.~~

Bachelor #2: Her Pregnant Agenda
Grant Lawson—The guy's a dead ringer for Pierce Brosnan—who wouldn't want to fall into his strong, protective arms!

Bachelor #3: Fill-in Fiancée
Brett Hamilton—The playboy from England is really a British lord! Can I find him a princess...or has he found her already?

Bachelor #4: Santa Brought a Son
Reed Connors—The ambitious VP seems to have a heavy heart. Only his true love could have broken it . But where is she now?

Bachelor #5: Rules of Engagement
Nate Leeman—Definitely a lone wolf kind of guy. A bit hard around the edges, but I'll bet there's a tender, aching heart inside.

Bachelor #6: One Bachelor To Go
Jack Devon—The guy is so frustratingly elusive. Arrogant and implacable, too! He's going last on my matchmaking list until I can figure out what kind of woman a mystery man like him prefers....

Chapter One

She was not going to cry.

Ariana Fitzpatrick rushed into the forty-ninth floor ladies' room of Wintersoft, Inc., found the place thankfully empty and slammed into the first stall. She shoved a Kleenex hard against her eyelids. No matter how rotten the day, no matter how guilty she felt, she would not cry. Not again. She was past the crying stage of pregnancy.

She glanced down at the seven-and-a-half-month protrusion around her middle and sniffled. "Way past the crying stage."

She sniffled again and leaned her throbbing head against the cool stall divider. Reaching for another tissue, she found the dispenser empty, and that was the straw that broke the camel's back.

Sobs ripped free like a mob at a soccer game. Once loose there was no stopping them. She, normally so professional and calm, cried until her headache became a concussion, her eyelids turned to puff pastry, and her throat felt like raw hamburger.

"I hate you Benjy Walburn," she blubbered, slamming one fist into the wall.

"Are you all right in there?" A voice called, and Ariana wished she were anywhere but here. She clapped a hand over her mouth and hiccuped.

Someone rapped on the stall. "Would you like to talk?"

"No." And that one word started the bawling over again.

"Open the door," a concerned voice demanded.

"Who is it?" Ariana managed to squeak.

"Emily Winters. Who's in there?"

If she wasn't already squalling her brains out, she'd cry. Emily Winters, the boss's daughter. The jig was up, the party was over. She may as well come clean. Besides, she was desperate for a tissue.

"Ariana Fitzpatrick," she said and stepped out, taking care not to whack her belly on anything in the process. She grabbed for the tissue dispenser.

"Ariana!" Emily's gaze flew to Ariana's midsection. "Are you all right?"

"Yes," she managed to say, which was a silly answer given that she clearly was not all right.

How could she explain to Emily Winters, of all people, the extent of her duplicity? Ariana battled another wave of tears. More than anything she didn't want to lose her job. Couldn't afford to lose it now with the babies coming and Benjy gone like the wind.

"Obviously, something has happened. If not your babies, then what?" In a chic blue sheath topped with a white jacket, Emily looked slim and professional. With the emphasis on slim.

Ariana was desperate to tell someone, was certain she would explode if she didn't. These months of white lies and saving face and fretting over possible damage to Wintersoft, Inc. had taken an enormous toll on her. Who better to hear the truth than the boss's tender-hearted daughter? Before the tears rolled again, she managed to blurt, "I'm a big fat liar."

With the emphasis on fat.

Emily didn't looked shocked, only concerned. "Want to tell me the problem? Maybe I can help."

"I'm pregnant."

"Well, uh—yes," Emily's sapphire gaze dropped to Ariana's middle filling up half the distance between the stall and the sink. "I had noticed that."

Ariana finally found her humor and laughed. Emily joined her. Who wouldn't notice a woman who'd swallowed a Volkswagen?

"I think everyone in the company is excited about your twins and the upcoming wedding."

Ariana fought back a new threat of tears. "That's the problem. There's not going to be a wedding. I made that up." The little white lie had seemed like the best solution at the time. "Benjy jilted me two months ago—on the day we were supposed to be married."

"Oh, Ariana, I'm so sorry." Emily ripped more tissue from the dispenser and poked the soft paper into Ariana's hand. "But I don't understand. Why lie about it? You're not the loser, he is."

Ariana sniffed and dabbed at her sodden face. One of the twins elbowed her. Taking the hint, she leaned sideways, giving him more room. "I love my babies and wouldn't undo them if I could. But I was worried about causing a problem for the company. My job in public relations is to make Wintersoft, Inc. look good.

Instead I'm a walking poster child for an abstinence program.''

At least that was part of the reason. She'd thought everything would eventually work itself out and the lie wouldn't matter, but the problem only grew until she didn't know what to do anymore.

"Nonsense. The company's image is not the important issue here, Ariana. You and your twins are." Emily frowned. "This Benjy jerk *is* planning to support you financially, isn't he?''

Ariana sighed and pressed the tissue into her burning eyes. "According to Benjy, I'm on my own. He thinks the stork brought these babies.''

"That's outrageous!''

The bathroom door swished open and Carmella Lopez entered. The older woman took one look at Ariana's tear-stained face and draped a motherly arm over her shoulders. "What's outrageous?''

Executive assistant to Emily's father, Carmella was way too close to the top of the pecking order for Ariana's comfort. She'd much rather Mr. Winters never know about her duplicity. But Emily spoke before Ariana could stop her. "Ariana's fiancé left her and refuses to support their babies.''

"The dog.'' Carmella stepped away, sympathetic brown eyes traveling over Ariana's very pregnant body. "What you need is a good lawyer.''

"As if I can afford one,'' Ariana bemoaned.

Eyes lighting up, Emily held up a finger. "I told you I could help. One of the best attorney's in Boston is our general counsel, and I'll bet we can talk him into taking your case pro bono.'' She took Ariana's hand and pulled her to the door.

"Oh, no, I couldn't.'' Ariana pulled back, horrified.

Wasn't being pregnant, unwed and jilted bad enough without becoming a charity case to boot?

"Of course you can. Lawyers do that kind of thing all the time. Ethics or something. And Grant Lawson is the embodiment of ethics." She gave another tug, and Ariana, already overbalanced, had no choice but to follow.

Carmella forestalled them. "Emily, could you come by my office later? We need to discuss an important matter." Some sort of mental message passed between the two women.

"Of course." Emily wiggled two fingers and pushed Ariana into the hall. "See you later."

Ariana had a stitch in her side by the time Emily escorted her up to the fiftieth floor, through the outer office and passed Mr. Lawson's prim and proper assistant, Sunny Robbins. After a soft knock, she poked her head around the door marked General Counsel. "Hi, Grant, do you have a minute? Ariana could use some advice."

Working furiously over a stack of papers, Grant Lawson glanced up at the interruption. He lay his pen aside. "Advice is what I do best. Come on in."

Athletically built with black hair and stunning blue eyes, all six foot two of Wintersoft's top attorney exuded strength and power. Mr. Perfect, as the girls in the secretarial pool called him, was gorgeous. Respected by everyone in the company, he was the object of more than one single female's fantasy. But while friendly and polite, he maintained a businesslike reserve that screamed, "Don't get too close."

Though aware of his good looks and impeccable manners, Ariana was not among the drooling. She was too busy falling for men who needed rescuing. Trouble was, she never succeeded in solving their problems; she only added to her own.

Rising, Grant came around the desk. "Have a seat, ladies."

They did. Emily sat with her long, slender legs crossed and her skirt at midthigh. Ariana envied anyone the ability to cross one leg over the other. Choosing the widest chair, she eased into the plush brown seat. Getting out of the thing might be another problem altogether.

"Ariana's ex-fiancé is refusing to pay child support," Emily said. "I told her you might be willing to take her case—pro bono, of course, since her fiancé has left her in such a difficult situation."

Grant leaned his backside against the desk and crossed his ankles. Ariana would bet a week's salary that suit was tailor-made to conform perfectly to his oh-so-fit physique. There ought to be a law against a man looking that good in the presence of an overly pregnant woman with a tear-blotched face.

"I'll need the details first, but I'm always happy to help a co-worker if I can."

"Good." Emily rose from the deep cushioned chair, graceful as you please. Ariana turned green with envy. "I'll leave you two to discuss the particulars." She squeezed Ariana's shoulder gently. "Everything will work out. Don't worry. You're in good hands."

With that she took her leave and Ariana was left to confess her total stupidity to Mr. Perfect. As the story unfolded, faint lines appeared in Grant's forehead. Occasionally he broke in with a question. Twice he nodded, his appraising gaze drifting over Ariana in a way that made her squirm. He probably thought she was an idiot.

When she finished, feeling that she'd dumped all her dirty laundry on the floor before him, Grant tapped one thumb against his lip, clearly thinking the matter over. A gold Rolex peeked from beneath perfectly white cuffs.

"So, Ariana— Do you mind if I call you that?"

"I'm feeling pretty old lately, but Ms. Fitzpatrick really does me in. Ariana would be great."

A tiny smile tipped the sides of his mouth. "And I'm Grant. Somehow you don't look like a Fitzpatrick. Irish, isn't it?"

The expression on his face said her tan skin and mahogany hair sharply contrasted with the image of an Irish woman.

"My dad is Irish. Mom is Cuban."

"Ah. That explains it. I'd wondered."

Ariana batted her eyes in surprise. Grant Lawson, aka Mr. Perfect, had wondered about her? She was seven and a half months pregnant with twins and a man like Grant had wondered about her? The teeny compliment lifted her spirits immeasurably.

"So tell me about this ex-fiancé." Grant resumed his relaxed posture, leaning on the desk. Ariana suspected he struck the stance as a means to disarm people and gain their confidence. His pose worked. Some of the tension eased from her shoulders, relieved to finally share her problems—and the truth—with someone in the company.

For weeks, ever since she'd waited three hours at the courthouse only to discover Benjy not only wasn't going to marry her, but he had moved in with a woman he'd been seeing for weeks, Ariana had propagated the myth that they were awaiting the twins' birth before tying the knot. Wintersoft had been good to her, giving her a chance in the competitive field of Public Relations, and the software company didn't deserve a tarnished image because of her.

"Benjy ran off the day we were supposed to be married."

"Benjy?" He cocked an eyebrow. "Is that your dog?"

She could tell he was kidding. "I wish. Then I could have taken him to the pound."

"Or had him put to sleep?"

Ariana laughed, surprised that the coolly aloof Grant Lawson had a sense of humor. She appreciated his efforts at levity. Anything to ease the awful strain she'd been under. "Unfortunately, Benjy is the father of my twins. The very absent, unconcerned father of my twins."

"He *is* a dog."

"More like a lap poodle. I only wished I'd recognized his penchant for expecting women to take care of him. And when I say women, I mean multiple women."

An instant change came over her new attorney. The cool pose stiffened. His top lip thinned to a narrow line. When he spoke, his voice was harsh. "He cheated on you?"

"I suppose I should have suspected it by the way he avoided making definite wedding plans, but I was clueless until he didn't show up at the courthouse. Even then, I worried he'd been in an accident." She gave a rueful laugh. "Stupid, huh?"

"You had a right to expect fidelity from the father of your children. Trust is an important part of a relationship."

The news of Benjy's betrayal had been a knife in

the back. She'd tried so hard to help him when he came out of rehab, but as soon as she was too pregnant to be his pretty little toy anymore, he found other play-mates. And she'd been too naive to recognize the symptoms. Admitting such a thing aloud, even to a lawyer, was humiliating.

"And what about you?" Grant pinned her with a courtroom gaze that would have quelled any witness. "Were you unfaithful?"

"Never." Ariana blushed at the blunt question. Though Benjy was not the first in a long line of bad relationships, he had been her first and only lover. She'd been so certain her love was all he needed to overcome his problems that she'd given herself to him completely.

Ariana's self-confidence suffered to know she'd been used, that Benjy had only wanted someone to take care of him while he got back on his feet. He'd never wanted to marry her. In fact, he'd been furious about the pregnancy and had even urged her to end it. But after a terrible fight, Benjy had done an about-face, asking her to marry him at some vague, future date.

Grant rocked away from the desk and stalked around to his chair. "I'll take your case."

Ariana batted her eyes in surprise.

Just like that? He'd take her case.

He yanked a legal pad from beneath a neat stack on his desk. "Mr. Poodle will do his part to look after your children. You have my word on that."

Grant furiously scribbled notes on the pad, letting his mind drift over the bits of information Ariana had shared. He did plenty of pro bono cases, especially for company employees, and he enjoyed doing them.

Those were the cases that made him feel like a true champion of the law, serving those in need. But he hadn't taken Ariana's case out of altruism, not totally anyway. If there was one thing he knew about it was ugly domestic cases in which one partner cheated the other and then tried to skip out scot-free. No one should have to live through that kind of pain.

He raised his eyes to the woman who knew exactly how that felt and was struck again by her smooth skin. Though every previous conversation had been business related, he'd noticed Ariana before. She was lovely. Almond-shaped eyes that defied him to name the color. And dark brown hair that floated around her shoulders with a rich, natural shine. Always warm and friendly even to the biggest jerks in the building, she had a dark beauty that would fascinate any man who still had a heart in his chest. Which left him out since a great gaping hole occupied the area in his rib cage where a heart once resided.

He tried not to look at her stomach—a near impossible task. He'd never seen anyone quite so pregnant. Behind the brave thrust of her chin and the steady gaze, he saw the tear-stained cheeks and detected the vulnerable quiver of her full lower lip. All his protective urges leaped to the fore. Urges he hadn't acknowledged for a long time. And though they disturbed him no little bit, he'd be hanged if this fiancé of hers got away without taking equal responsibility for those children.

"Do you know this Benjy character's current address?"

"I know where he works." She gave him the address. "But don't expect him to be cooperative."

The idea angered him. What kind of worthless scum refused to acknowledge his own offspring? Children didn't deserve to be pawns in domestic litigation. If he'd been fortunate enough to have a child...

He put the brakes on that thought immediately. Just as he'd closed the door on love, he'd promised not to dwell on what could never be.

He pushed a pad toward Ariana. "Will you write that address down? Along with the correct spelling of Mr. Walburn's name?"

The element of surprise was always important in these cases, so he needed to make certain he had every last detail, right down to the correct spellings. He was nothing if not thorough.

Ariana gripped the chair arms and rocked several times, her off-center body not cooperating. When he started to offer his assistance, she held up one hand to stop him, and shook her head. "I can do this."

She rocked again and then again. On the next try she stood. Hiding a smile, Grant exhaled, unaware he'd been holding his breath. Her stubbornness appealed to him.

He watched her move toward the desk, a light green dress billowing softly around her legs. Except for the enormous midsection, Ariana Fitzpatrick was actually very small and graceful. Tiny hands, slim shoulders, fine-boned, heart-shaped face with the kindest eyes he'd ever seen. An odd twist wrenched his gut. Sympathy pains surely, though he wasn't prone to such feelings. A man couldn't find a woman appealing when she was pregnant with someone else's baby. Could he?

Absolutely not.

Taking the pen, Ariana leaned over the paper. Her hair spilled forward, inches from his nose. He inhaled—purely a function of normal biology—and filled his lungs with the faint scent of flowers. Gardenias, he thought.

Nature forced another breath. Ah, lovely. So clean and fresh. He studied her profile, admiring the graceful angle of her neck, waiting for the moment she lifted her head so that he could study her delicate face more closely. Purely for professional reasons, of course. An attorney gained a lot of information from a client's eyes.

As she straightened, her naturally dark complexion paled, and she grabbed for the edge of the desk.

"Whoa," she whispered and weaved sideways, knocking his nameplate to the beige carpet.

Grant was out of his chair and around the desk faster than a guilty criminal could say appeal. He slipped an arm around her middle and had the novel experience of feeling a stomach move beneath his fingertips.

Instead of the aversion he'd expected, his own stomach quivered in awed response. He shook off the sensation. Sentimentality had no place in attorney-client relations.

"Are you all right?" His voice sounded gruff.

"Fine." She panted a few times, then took a deep breath. "A little dizzy. That's all."

He backed her to the chair and very gingerly eased her down, then remained standing in front of her, studying the pale line around her mouth. "Has this happened before?"

A little pink tongue flicked out over dry lips. She closed her eyes and let her head fall back. "Occasionally."

Along one wall he kept a small refrigerator stocked with drinks—one of his perks as head attorney. Keeping one eye on Ariana, he went to it and retrieved a bottle of water. Uncapping the container, he held the drink to her lips. Her eyes fluttered open.

"Thanks." Her voice was a whisper. She took the water and sipped.

"Are you eating properly?"

She hedged. "Today was a bad day."

Placing a hand on each chair arm, he bent low and peered into her eyes. "What did you eat?"

She sat up straighter. "I'm fine now."

"I don't think so. You're still pale. Are you getting prenatal care? Taking vitamins? Sleeping enough?"

Her slender shoulders stiffened. She shrank back from him and in a soft voice said, "Am I on trial here?"

"I beg your pardon." He relented, leaning back slightly, though remaining close enough to notice the lines of fatigue around her eyes and mouth. What if she fainted and slithered out of the chair? He glanced at his watch. Time to go home anyway. "I'll escort you to your car whenever you're ready to leave."

She shook her head slightly. "I rode the T."

Of course she had. What was he thinking? Most everyone in Boston used public transportation, even him, though lately he'd taken to driving his car because of the erratic work hours. Fortunately, another of his perks was an underground parking space.

He had a car and she didn't. And she was unwell.

One glance at this Rolex and Grant made a quick decision, his usual kind. "That settles it."

"Settles what?"

"I'm driving you home."

"Grant, you're very thoughtful." Ariana recapped the water and placed the bottle on his desk. "But I'm fine now—really—and perfectly capable of seeing myself home.''

"This has nothing to do with kindness and everything to do with common sense. You're exhausted, hungry, and you nearly fainted. You have no business on public transportation. What if you pass out? As a gentlemen I would be remiss not to see you safely home.'' He offered his hands, palms up. "Let's go.''

She drew back, stubborn chin lifting. "I need a lawyer, not a keeper.''

He waited, offer still open. Couldn't she understand that he knew best? "You'd risk your babies out of stubbornness?''

Ariana fisted both small hands on her thighs. She was getting her Irish up, an attitude he found intriguing. "That was a dirty trick.''

He allowed a tiny smile and shrugged. "I'm an attorney. What did you expect?''

Ariana's full mouth pursed as she thought over the offer. "Well…I am a little weak in the knees. And the T will be standing room only.''

"Air-conditioned car. No jostling bodies.'' He loved negotiations.

Finally she poked a finger at him—a small, stub-nailed finger. "Not that I normally need anyone to take care of me, but okay, you win—this time.''

Suppressing a laugh, Grant helped her out of the chair. Didn't she understand? He always won.

Chapter Two

With considerable pleasure, Emily Winters watched Ariana and her new attorney exit the building together. She felt like that legendary Samaritan performing the good deed for the day. Grant, with his take-charge attitude and legal genius, would look after sweet Ariana. If anyone could squeeze support out of that deadbeat fiancé, Grant could.

With a contented smile she headed for Carmella's office. As vice president of Global Sales, Emily had plenty to do, but if Carmella wanted to see her, something important concerning their "secret project" must have developed.

"Have you read this?" Carmella asked as soon as Emily entered her office. Displaying the cover of a romance novel, she then pressed the book to her bosom. "This story is so romantic. Just like Matt and Sarah."

"Everything did work out for the best with those two, didn't it?" Regardless of Emily's discomfort with the whole idea of matchmaking, once the brainy accountant noticed his sweet, innocent secretary there was no stopping the inevitable.

"Ah, if only the others were so easy." Carmella lay aside the book and tilted her head, salt and pepper hair catching the gleam of light. "So, is Grant Lawson to be the next lucky bachelor?"

"Grant? Oh, you mean with Ariana?" Emily shook her head. "The idea never crossed my mind. When I heard Ariana crying in the bathroom and discovered the reason why, my heart broke for her."

"So, this is not part of our plan to see another of your father's bachelor employees joined in happy matrimony?"

Emily sighed. Ever since Carmella had come to her with the distressing news that her father wanted her to marry yet another of the firm's bachelors, she'd been forced into the uncomfortable roll of matchmaker. If she didn't find wives for Wintersoft's eligible men, her father would publicly embarrass himself and everyone else by prodding the bachelors in *her* direction. He'd done that once already, and the resulting marriage and divorce had left Emily willing to do most anything, right down to prying into other people's affairs, to avoid suffering that humiliation again. She knew her father well and once he got an idea in his head, he was like a dog on a bone. Anything she might say to try to change his mind was wasted breath, so she had no choice but to resort to playing the reluctant matchmaker.

"No, Carmella, I'm not setting Ariana and Grant up with each other. Ariana really needs Grant's help."

"And you really need Grant to find a wife."

"Other than me."

"Exactly."

Carmella patted her hand. "Your father loves you very much, Emily. He only wants your happiness."

"And ten or twelve grandchildren."

Carmella laughed. "Would one or two be so bad?"

"Someday maybe, but not now. Until he realizes that I can run this company as good as any man, my career is my primary focus. I know my father loves me, and I adore him, too, but he has a blind spot where I'm concerned. As long as one male employee remains unattached, he's a candidate for my hand in marriage." Her father would see to that. "And on that note, how is the research going on the remaining bachelors?"

"Nothing at all on Jack Devon." Two lines formed between Carmella's eyebrows as she studied the computer screen. "He's a rather mysterious creature."

"What about the very British and ultrahandsome Brett Hamilton? Maybe we should research him next."

"Whatever we do, we'd better hurry. How much longer can you keep your father believing that story about your new beau?"

Emily gnawed her lip, truly worried. If her father found out that her latest boyfriend was actually her dear and completely gay friend, Stephen, he'd be back in action, pressing his unmarried employees to pursue her. And she planned to make sure that never happened again.

Ariana followed Grant through the cool, dim belly of the building into the parking garage, her sensible flats echoing against the concrete. With legs twice as long as hers, Grant slowed his gait to accommodate her much slower pace. Given the cargo she carried, the gesture warmed her, though she imagined Grant Lawson always did the proper thing in any situation.

"Here we are." He raised a key ring and pointed. Security system disengaged and locks snicked open on a gleaming bronze Lexus.

Ariana tried not to gape. She should have expected him to drive a fancy car, but she'd never ridden in one before. Neither her blue-collar roots, nor her current salary included such luxuries.

Grant proceeded her, opened the door, and gently settled her into the seat before pressing the door closed with a quiet click. Even if Benjy had remembered to open the door, he would have slammed her skirt in it. Or maybe her hand. And then groused about how women wanted to be liberated, but still expected a man to wait on them hand and foot. Yeah, right. As if Benjy had ever brought her so much as a glass of water.

Her brain caught on the thought. Grant, only a workplace acquaintance, had instinctively brought her a drink of water and offered her a ride home. He'd shown her more kindness and courtesy in the last half hour than Benjy had in over a year of dating. What an idiot she'd been.

Keenly aware of her pathetic taste in the opposite sex, Ariana slithered down into the seat. She'd beaten herself up enough for one day, and so, for the moment, she forced the thought away and wallowed in the luxury of Grant's Lexus. Soft, luxurious ivory leather. Real walnut wood trim. And a dashboard with so many gadgets and computers, she'd almost swear the car could fly.

Grant slid into the driver's seat, subtly mixing his expensive sandalwood scent with the smell of fine leather. The engine hummed to life at his touch and the glorious vehicle whispered out of the parking space.

As they pulled onto the crowded street, Grant slipped

a pair of designer sunglasses into place, effectively covering his stunning blue eyes.

Though the seats were butter soft, Ariana squirmed to find a comfortable position. Having two babies in a space made for one didn't leave a mom much room.

She rubbed a hand down one side, pushing someone's foot out of the way as an upbeat country tune issued from the sound system. Alan Jackson sang about driving his first car.

"You're a country music fan?"

"Um-hmm." Grant maneuvered the car around an exhaust belching bus. "Why? Surprised?"

"Somehow you don't seem the type."

"I have fairly eclectic taste." He motioned to a CD case. "Take a look. Choose what you like."

She flipped through the stacks, finding every conceivable type of music. Classics, jazz, rock, country, Gaelic.

"This is quite a variety."

"I aim to please." He draped a wrist over the leather-clad steering wheel. A shaft of October sunlight reflected off his Rolex.

Ah. Now she understood. The variety was for his passengers' pleasure. Clients, she wondered? Or women?

Neither was one bit her business, but the idea of Grant Lawson's women piqued her interest. What type did he like? Sophisticated? Intellectual? Naughty or nice? According to the office grapevine, Grant kept his private life to himself.

Ariana couldn't believe she was thinking such a thing. She was about to be a mother, for heaven's sakes. The opposite sex held no appeal for her at this juncture in life. And given her track record and the fact that she had no sense whatsoever concerning men, she would do well never to fall for another one.

Not that she had any such thoughts about Grant. He was doing her a favor out of kindness. She was not interested in him as a man. Only as an attorney.

"Well, which shall it be?"

Had he read her thoughts? She gulped, aware that a dark blush heated her neck.

"Excuse me?"

His lips quirked. "Have you selected your favorite music?"

"Oh." Flustered, she handed him the Gaelic CD.

He scanned the title, then lifted an eyebrow. "Good choice."

She smiled and slathered on a thick brogue. "What did ye expect from an Irish lass? We love our bonny fiddle music."

"What about your Latin half?"

"Ah, you should see me clog to a rumba."

As soon as she said the words, they both glanced toward her middle, caught each other's eyes and laughed. Ariana knew how ridiculous she'd look doing any kind of energetic dance.

"Maybe I'll leave my clogging shoes on the shelf for a few more weeks. Right now, the twins are doing enough clogging for all of us."

"When is your due date?" he asked.

The personal question didn't bother Ariana. After all, Grant was her attorney, ready to fight for her support from Benjy. He needed to know these things. And he was a nice guy, a man she instinctively trusted.

"Six more weeks. The babies are due right before Thanksgiving." She fidgeted in the seat, turned sideways to face him and pointed to a panel on the dash. "Do you mind if I ask you what that is?"

"GPS. Navigation system."

"How does it work?"

He pressed a button. "Give me your address and I'll show you."

As she quoted the street and number, he tapped in the information. "The computer will automatically map the route."

"Amazing."

"Interesting toy, but I seldom use it."

"You never get lost?"

He shot her a look. "Never."

Ariana suppressed a giggle. Men were so funny about that.

They rode along for a while without talking, the lively music filling the space between them. Outside the tinted windows, the New England autumn was showing off. Bright evening sunshine backlit a glorious display of orange, red and yellow foliage. Ariana breathed in a contented sigh. The radical change of seasons was what she enjoyed most about living in Boston.

Then the car slowed and Ariana looked up to discover they were nowhere near her apartment. A touch of anxiety zipped up her arms. Protectively, she bracketed her belly with both arms.

"I thought you never got lost?"

Behind the sunglasses, his look was indulgent. "We aren't lost. We're at a quiet little restaurant that serves great food. You are hungry, aren't you?"

"Yes, but this isn't necessary. I can cook at home. In fact, I have to cook. I promised Roger."

Grant killed the engine and turned in the seat, draping one arm over the steering wheel. His gaze flickered to her stomach. "You have a date?"

"Well, not a real date. Roger lives in my building and I cook for him a couple of nights a week."

"Ah. I see." Clearly he didn't. "Tell you what." He handed her a cell phone. "You call Roger and offer to bring him carry-out instead. Then, we'll have a pleasant dinner while I gather some more information about your case."

Ariana knew he was only being considerate and he did need more details to effectively represent her, but she was far more accustomed to giving than receiving. Besides, Roger looked forward to their time together. "I hate to disappoint him. He's really a dear man."

Seeing her hesitation, Grant said, "Give me his number. I'll call and make certain he's agreeable. Surely he'll understand the need for you to meet with your attorney."

She reached for the cell phone with a resigned sigh. Obviously Grant Lawson was a man who liked to have his way. Given the ache in her back and the wobble in her knees, she'd go along with his wishes this once. "I'll let him know he has carry-out on the way."

"That works for me." Turning, he exited the car and came around to her side while she spoke on the phone, then escorted her into the restaurant.

"I hope you like Italian." Grant pushed open the door to Gionni's, inhaling the rich spiced air as Ariana preceded him inside. He liked the quaint Italian restaurant snuggled into a space right off the alley where only the locals would find it. Checkered cloths on the tables, a breadboard and knife waiting for the fresh, hot loaf that would appear the moment they sat down, La Boheme playing softly in the background. The old-world atmosphere soothed him after a difficult day. He hoped the place would work its magic for Ariana as well. For all her pretense to the contrary, she was frazzled.

"Mmm. This is lovely." Ariana gazed around, and Grant relaxed, pleased that she appreciated his choice.

The hostess showed them to a corner table, and Grant seated Ariana, once more catching the faint scent of gardenias.

She adjusted her chair to accommodate her enlarged stomach, and he marveled at a woman's ability to deal with the changes of pregnancy. Physically, financially, emotionally, the total burden of childbearing rested on a single mother, a fact that disturbed his sense of fair play.

"This place smells delicious. What do you recommend?" she asked, smiling.

Grant noted how full and soft her lips appeared. She had a beautiful smile, brilliant white against her dark complexion. Orthodontia must have cost her family a fortune.

He opened his menu. "If you like Italian, there are no bad choices. I'm having linguini with pesto sauce."

"That sounds good. I'll have that, too."

"And antipasto. You need the vegetables."

Closing her menu with a soft *wap,* she tilted her head appraisingly. "Are you always so bossy?"

He smiled, liking the way her hazel eyes flashed. "Yes."

She laughed, a warm melody, and he liked that, too. "All right. Antipasto."

"Mineral water or milk?"

She stuck out her tongue and grimaced. "Plain water."

The waiter, who appeared to have enjoyed more than his share of Gionni's fine cooking, took their order and moved away.

Lacing his fingers, Grant propped both forearms on the table and leaned forward. As long as he had Ariana in his company, he might as well make the most of their time. "Will you be uncomfortable if we discuss your case during dinner?"

"Of course not. I thought that was the purpose for stopping here."

It was, wasn't it? The fact that he enjoyed her company and liked looking at a pretty face was an added bonus. And she certainly had no business standing on her feet cooking for this Roger person. The very idea annoyed him. Roger annoyed him. And Ariana's devotion to the man annoyed him even more. He'd heard the sweet tone of her voice when she'd made that phone call—the sincere apology, and the promise of tomorrow night. If he had his way, she wouldn't go out with the loser at all. Hadn't she learned anything from her experience with that mutt, Benjy?

"Have you considered that your ex-fiancé may deny paternity?"

Ariana's eyes widened. "Could he do such a thing?"

Grant opened his palms in a questioning gesture. "You know him better than I do."

She lay a protective hand over her abdomen. "Benjy does whatever makes him happy at the moment. And spending money on anyone except himself does not make him happy."

"We're likely looking at a court case, then."

Ariana frowned, gnawing at her lush bottom lip. "Isn't there another way? Benjy's been out of rehab less than a year. I wouldn't want to be the cause of a relapse.''

Grant couldn't believe this woman. Her fiancé had left her in dire straits and she was concerned about upsetting him? ''Taking responsibility for one's actions is a part of adulthood.''

''I know.'' She took a deep breath and nodded. ''You're right. My babies deserve that much.''

''Is there any chance that he might file for custody?''

''Benjy?'' The light came back on in her face. ''He wouldn't take custody of a parakeet if it required any sacrifice.''

He hoped she was right. Men had a way of behaving strangely when a woman pressed them for support.

''Okay. We'll file the paternity suit and ask for full custody with child support. But what are your plans in the meantime? The case may take a while, depending on how quickly we locate your ex. Financially speaking, can you afford medical care? Child care? Do you have family here in Boston that can help you after the twins are delivered?''

She shook her head, shiny hair dancing around her shoulders. ''My family lives in Florida.''

''All of them? You're completely alone in this?'' He didn't much like the sound of that. ''Would your mother consider coming to Boston for a few weeks until you adjust to some sort of schedule?''

''Oh, no. Absolutely not. I have friends who will help out, but I can't let Mama come here.''

He frowned at that. ''I take it you and your family are not close.''

His own family was small—Mom, Dad and a married sister in Connecticut, but if he needed them—

which he never did—they'd be here as fast as Dad's Lincoln would go.

"But that's the problem. We're very close. That's why I haven't told them."

The idea shocked him. He leaned back in his chair and stared at her fragile little face. "Your family doesn't know about your pregnancy?"

"No. It would break Mama's heart."

"To be a grandmother?"

"Of course not. Mama loves kids, but she already has enough grandchildren. My brother has two and my sister has three."

"Then what's the problem?"

Their meal arrived. Ariana gave the waiter a warm smile and thanked him while Grant waited patiently for her answer. She might be trying to avoid the subject, but he was an attorney and never forgot the question.

The pungent smell of pesto wrapped around the table. From the depths of the restaurant came the low murmur of voices—some in Italian—and the gentle strains of an Italian aria.

Ariana adjusted her napkin and took a bite of the linguini. With a deep sigh, she briefly closed her eyes. "Wonderful," she breathed.

He concurred, savoring the rich flavor while appreciating Ariana's impeccable manners, and the dainty way her fingers tore the bread into small chunks. She popped a piece into her mouth and chewed, making a soft moaning sound. A thought filtered through his mind that had nothing whatsoever to do with Italian food.

Good grief. The woman was pregnant. Explosively so.

He swallowed, eager to escape his wicked thoughts. "And your reasons for keeping the secret would be?"

"You're very persistent, aren't you?"

"Bossy, persistent, stubborn. Any of those adjectives apply. Answer the question, please." There. He felt much more like an attorney. "Why haven't you told your family about the babies? Are you ashamed of them?"

"No!" Changeable hazel eyes darkened with anger. "My twins are the best thing that has ever happened to me, and I won't allow anyone to look down on them because their father is a loser and their mother is a bad judge of character."

"I beg your pardon." Without thinking, Grant reached across the table and wrapped his hand around hers. The warm velvet skin jolted him, but he held on, determined to make amends. He'd brought her here to help, not to hurt her. "Please. I was in no way demeaning your situation. Children are a gift, no matter the particulars of their conception."

God knew how much he'd once wanted such a gift in his life.

Ariana glanced down at their touching hands, then carefully slipped her fingers from beneath his. "Apology accepted."

Eyes downcast, she busied herself with a sip of water.

"So, are you going to tell me why you haven't informed your family about the imminent arrival of two new grandchildren that you clearly treasure? Children aren't something you can hide forever."

Her lips twitched, lips that glistened from the oil and vinegar dressing. His gut reacted. She had a beautiful mouth that drew a man's attention. Stupid Benjy. How had he resisted her?

"All right. If you insist." She dabbed those sensational lips with the cheery red napkin. "But it's a long story."

"I'm in no hurry." He'd left work much earlier than usual because of Ariana, but had no previous plans for tonight other than spending an hour or so at the health club. Other than the occasional date or dinners with his family, most weekdays found him chained to a desk until well into the evening.

"Mama and her brother, Uncle Ernesto, escaped Cuba as teenagers. They arrived here in a boat, tired, hungry, scared, and speaking only Spanish."

"Your mother is an illegal?"

Ariana laughed. "Don't ever say that to Mama. She is the proudest naturalized citizen in the entire state of Florida. And whatever you do, don't get into an American history quiz with her. She'll wax you."

Though he doubted he'd ever meet the woman, Grant admired that kind of strength and determination. Having grown up in a very comfortable home, he'd never considered how blessed he was to live in the land of the free. He couldn't imagine the difficulties of coming to a strange country to begin a new life.

"But how does her immigration relate to your pregnancy?"

"I'm getting there." With a little wait-a-minute wave of dainty hands, Ariana sipped her water again, then continued. "Daddy is a fishing guide. Mama worked for many years as a domestic. With three children, finances were always tight, but Mama held on to the dream that her children would go to college and climb the ladder to success. Sean and Marisa had no such interest, so it fell to me as the oldest to make Mama's dream come true."

The music drifting through the restaurant changed to an accordion beat. Dishes clattered somewhere in the background, but all Grant's attention focused on Ariana. There was more to her than a pretty face and a pregnant body. He knew about family expectations, having fallen far short of the dream his father had had for him. Even now, he continued to disappoint, a truth that wore away at his conscience as aggressively as his flamboyant father wore away at a jury.

"Didn't you want to attend college?" Waiting for her reply he took a bite of the antipasto, the garlic flavor invigorating his taste buds, even as the conversation with Ariana invigorated his other senses.

"For as long as I can remember. And you should have seen Mama's face on the day I graduated. She was so beautiful, absolutely radiant with joy." Ariana's eyes lit up in remembrance. "She gave a party for everyone in our neighborhood and spent the entire day showing off my diploma and saying, 'Look, my Ariana, she is so smart. She will be somebody.'"

A faint Spanish lilt crept into Ariana's voice as she imitated her mother. Grant smiled, enjoying the sound.

"And even though she didn't want me to move so far away, she was thrilled when I landed the job at Wintersoft. And she is absolutely certain that someday I will be the public relations consultant for some movie star or maybe even the president."

"Is that what you want?"

Ariana's slender shoulders rolled forward in a shrug. "I love my job, and I want Mama to be proud. That's what really matters."

"I don't see how your pregnancy interferes with any

of that. Women with children continue to succeed in today's business world. Surely your mother understands that.''

''Ah, but there's more. You see, Mama's younger sister, Lily, had a stroke last year. Since most of Mama's relatives are still in Cuba, she and Lily are very close. Doctors wanted to put her in a nursing home, but Mama wouldn't hear of such a thing. So she and Daddy took Lily into their home, and Mama provides total care for her. The stress is enormous, but to Mama, caring for Lily is a labor of love. She has to do it.''

''And you don't want to add to your mother's worry?''

''Exactly. Mama would be torn between her need to be with Lily and her maternal desire to help her unwed, very pregnant and alone, daughter.'' Ariana's animated expression disappeared. She twisted a strand of linguini with her fork, stirring the food around the plate. ''It's bad enough that my children won't have a father, but now I will be a single mother struggling to make ends meet, instead of working my way up the ladder. I can't add that load of worry onto my already overburdened mother.''

Grant took a bite of his pasta and savored the spicy flavor as he mulled over Ariana Fitzpatrick's dilemma. She not only had the total responsibility of two unborn children, but all the hopes and dreams and concerns of her family rested on her fragile shoulders. And she believed she'd failed them.

''Ariana,'' he said gently. ''Sooner or later, your family will have to be told. You can't keep two babies a secret forever.''

''I know.'' She pulled in a ragged sigh. ''I know. In

fact, I really meant to all along, but first I wanted to get married—Mama's old-fashioned about that. I'd told the entire family about the engagement, but Benjy was always vague about the wedding date, not making a commitment until three days before the courthouse fiasco. I'd planned to let them know about the babies once we married. When that never happened and I had to tell them about the breakup, I couldn't bring myself to reveal the pregnancy at the same time. One shock was enough. But the longer I put off telling them, the harder it became.''

''Procrastination's hell.'' He should know. Hadn't he said he'd ''think about'' that high-profile position with his dad's law firm instead of refusing straight off the way he'd wanted to?

''No kidding. But once the babies come and I have my life under control again, everything will be fine and I'll announce them to the world. Oh, Grant, I love these babies so much. My soul sings every time I think of watching them grow from perfect babies into beautiful, unique individuals. I can't wait to hold them and count their fingers and kiss their noses and—'' One nail-chewed hand flew to her mouth. ''I'm sorry. You didn't ask for all that motherly gushing.''

Some odd emotion caught in his chest at Ariana's passionate speech. He'd dreamed of seeing that expression on Tiffany's face, of sharing the unbridled joy of pregnancy and childbirth with the woman he loved. But Tiffany had put an end to such foolish fantasies.

Carefully, deliberately, he shifted his attention back to a woman who did want children. As an attorney he empathized to a certain point with all his clients, but Ariana didn't appear to want his sympathy. Though she'd made some mistakes, she didn't wallow in self-pity, and, unlike her ex-fiancé, Ariana took full responsibility for her life, embracing the good parts of a difficult situation. He admired that. Yes, that was it. He admired her grit and determination. And he'd darn well find a way to see her through this difficult period.

He was still contemplating the particulars of such action, when the rotund waiter approached the table. "Sir, would you and the wife care for some dessert?"

Not wanting to embarrass the waiter, Grant ignored the mistake and shook his head. "None for me. Ariana?"

"No, thank you." He could see that she was disconcerted by the waiter's presumption that they were married. She dipped her head and fiddled with the remaining linguini, a pose he found both lovely and alluring. Long, dark eyelashes curved over the crests of her delicate, pink-tinged cheekbones.

For a moment he let his mind slide into the thought planted by the hapless waiter and the memories of Tiffany's cruelty. What if Ariana were his wife? What if those were his babies she carried beneath her heart? Regardless of Tiffany's taunts, he'd yearned to be a father, a good one. To take his children to the Cape and teach them to sail. Or to deep-sea fish and dig clams. Ariana would look beautiful walking barefoot along a sun-kissed beach with her rich, dark hair blowing in the breeze.

"Your check, sir." The waiter's voice pulled him out of his reverie. Swallowing thickly, he forced his gaze away from Ariana's lovely profile and reached for his wallet.

Teeth clenched, he reminded himself that the case

against marriage was settled long ago. As much as the truth pained him, there would be no children for Grant Lawson. And certainly no wife. Never, never, never a wife.

Chapter Three

Ariana shuffled work from the in-box to the out-box, wondering if she'd ever find the bottom of her desk. Exhausted, she wasn't sure how much longer she could handle the stress of the job, the stress of her situation, and the physical overload of carrying two championship wrestlers around her middle. Last night's quiet dinner had been an oasis, a momentary relief, that she'd needed badly. More than once today she'd wanted to cross the hallway to Grant Lawson's office and express her appreciation. Discretion and work held her back. Grant was a good guy, willing to do a fellow employee a huge favor. End of story. Never mind that she couldn't stop thinking about how much she'd enjoyed his company last evening.

A shadow fell across Ariana's desk. A tall shadow that smelled like expensive sandalwood. Peeking from beneath her eyelashes, she glimpsed well-groomed nails, a Rolex watch, and immaculate cuffs. She lifted her head, up, up, up, to find a pair of blue eyes boring into her. The babies reacted, shooting a karate chop to her backbone. What was it about blue eyes that made them behave that way?

"Are you ready?"

"For what?"

Grant tilted an eyebrow toward the clock hanging over the water cooler. "It's after five. Time to go home."

"So it is." One of the other girls in the department hadn't felt well this afternoon, and Ariana had taken over a project for her. She went back to proofreading the copy she'd spent the last hour and half writing, expecting Grant to go away.

He didn't.

Laying her yellow pencil aside, she asked, "Did you need something?"

"Go ahead and finish up." He crossed one arm over his middle and gripped his chin, stroking a thumb over his bottom lip. "I'll wait."

"For what?"

He tilted his thumb toward her. "For you to finish so I can drive you to your apartment."

Ariana lay both palms against her desk and rolled backward. "Are we going to have this argument again?"

It wasn't that she didn't appreciate the ride home. She did. The ride didn't disturb her. Grant did. He smelled too good, looked too perfect, and was far too thoughtful. And right now, her life was too much of a mess to think such things.

"No argument required. Since I drive near your neighborhood on my way home, dropping you off makes perfect sense. A crowded and noisy subway can't be healthy for unborn children."

"And what would you know about the needs of babies?" She was sorry the moment she spoke. A flicker of some pained emotion flashed in Grant's eyes and disappeared, leaving blue ice behind. She'd hurt his feelings. And Ariana would rather lie to the Supreme Court than hurt anyone.

"I'll need to drop this by Mr. Winter's office on the way out, but I accept your kind offer—on one condition."

He straightened in surprise. "And that would be...?"

"Dinner. At my place." She smiled, feeling much more in control of the situation and the funny twinges that occurred whenever Grant appeared. "I don't take favors without returning them."

"I took you to Gionni's because I wanted to."

"And I want to fix dinner for you."

"All right." He returned the smile, and darn if those tilted lips and crinkled eyes didn't cause another set of funny twinges. "You have discovered my weakness. Since I mostly eat out, I never pass up a home-cooked meal."

Ariana was aghast. He always ate out? "How does lasagna sound?"

"Perfect. And afterward, I have something to discuss with you."

"About my case?" Ariana gathered the copy and slipped the papers into a manila folder marked, Global Sales Ads. Locking her desk, she took her purse and came around to where Grant stood. "Did you locate Benjy?"

"Yes." Grant lightly placed two fingers against her back and guided her down the hallway, slowing his steps so she could take her time.

A feeling of foreboding sent goose bumps over Ariana's arms. The fact that he didn't elaborate bothered her some. If Grant's hand hadn't felt so good against her back, she'd have worried. But what was there to worry about? A part of her really didn't want anything from Benjy. Sure, he had a responsibility to the twins, but if she could afford to support them on her own, she would. Benjy and the word responsibility didn't quite go together.

The sleek Lexus wound through the city past roaring buses and honking cabbies. Ariana relaxed against the smooth interior, grateful to be in the climate controlled confines of Grant's car once again. She was tired. Her back hurt. Tilting her head against the headrest, she closed her eyes. The calming strains of "Für Elise" filtered from the CD player. Her last memory was of turning onto Beacon Street.

"Ariana." A gentle, masculine voice sounded close to her ear. A strong hand touched her shoulder. "Ariana. Wake up."

Such a nice dream. She inclined her head, capturing the hand between her cheek and shoulder. Such a nice hand, so strong and tender.

"We're here."

Ariana roused then, aware of her surroundings and of Grant Lawson's warm scent inches from her nose. Her eyes fluttered open. Sure enough. Grant's blue eyes glittered in amusement.

"Did I fall asleep?" she asked, sitting up straighter though she could no more escape his nearness than she could run a hundred yard dash. From this distance she noted his five o'clock shadow, a rather appealing darkness along his upper lip.

He tilted away, and she breathed a sigh, whether of

relief or pleasure, she didn't know. Catlike, she arched her shoulders and stretched, refreshed from the brief nap.

Grant opened her door and she stepped out of the car. A gentle breeze tugged at her hair and rattled the tree leaves overhead.

Inside the first floor of the brownstone, as they started up the stairs, a door to the right opened. A curly gray head popped out.

"Is that you, Ariana?"

"Hello, Mrs. Porter. Yes, it's me."

Her landlady bustled out into the entryway. "That Benjy fellow came by today."

Ariana's stomach lurched. What she didn't need right now was a confrontation with Benjy. "What did he want?"

"How should I know? I never liked that man." Mrs. Porter fluttered her hands. "I told him you moved."

With a laugh, Ariana wrapped the older woman in a hug. "You are my guardian angel."

"You need one." Mrs. Porter patted Ariana's belly. "And so do these babies." She caught sight of Grant then, standing quietly behind Ariana. Pointing one birdlike finger she asked, "And who is this?"

"This is my attorney. Grant Lawson meet Mrs. Pearl Porter, my landlady and unofficial watchdog."

Mrs. Porter pshawed as Grant took her tiny spotted hand in his long, lean one. "It's a pleasure meeting you, Mrs. Porter."

"High time this girl had someone to stand up for her." Her gray curls bobbed. "Always doing for everyone else, but never a thought for herself."

"Oh, Mrs. Porter." Once her landlady began extolling her virtues, the situation could get downright embarrassing.

"Don't 'oh' me. I'm telling the truth, and you know it." Her black eyes focused on Grant. "Last spring a bunch of hoodlums started hanging out at our neighborhood park. And what did Ariana do? She went down there every evening to watch the children, sat on the bench until dark, and every time one of those thugs showed up, she'd call the police. Pretty soon they decided our park wasn't worth the effort and went somewhere else. Can you imagine? A little thing like Ariana taking on a gang of hoodlums?"

Heat crept up Ariana's neck. "Really, Mrs. Porter. Anyone would have done the same."

"But 'anyone' didn't. You did. And what about that halfway house?" Mrs. Porter slowed long enough to shudder, and Ariana jumped at the opportunity to make an escape before she bored Grant to death. The halfway house was not a good subject right now.

"Do you know if Roger is home?"

Her landlady looked taken aback for a moment at the rapid change of subjects. "Uh, yes. I don't believe he's gone out at all today."

"Well, if you'll excuse us then. I promised Roger dinner and a game of checkers."

"A pleasure meeting you, Mrs. Porter."

"The feeling is mutual, I'm sure." The landlady leaned toward Ariana and in a stage whisper said, "He's the best one you've ever brought home. Could be a keeper."

Ariana rolled her eyes and laughed, hoping the comment wouldn't send Grant rushing out to his Lexus. She needed to repay his kindness as much as she wanted to know what he'd discussed with Benjy today.

Perhaps their conversation would offer a clue to why Benjy had come by the apartment after a two-month silence.

After a final round of goodbyes, she ascended the stairs, acutely aware of Grant's fingertips steadying her from behind.

At the third floor, Ariana led the way down the narrow hall to her apartment. Grant took the key from her—a novel experience—and unlocked the door.

Anxiety pinched at her. She wasn't exactly Martha Stewart around the house and her outside interests kept her on the go and too busy to worry much about how the place looked. Until now.

Grant's gaze roamed over the small living-dining room, taking in the orange and brown afghan tossed over the arm of the sofa, the stack of magazines on the coffee table, and this morning's coffee cup resting on the oval rug beside the couch. "Very homey."

Ariana laughed. She was who she was. No use trying to pretend otherwise. "My mother would cringe if she saw this place. And I'd be grounded for a month until everything was in tip-top shape."

Grant returned her smile. "I like it. It's relaxing."

"Good. Then make yourself at home. Watch TV or whatever. I'll put dinner on and give Roger a call." With one hand, she pulled a casserole dish from the freezer and reached for the telephone with the other.

Grant made no move toward the living area. "Are you sure you want me here when your date arrives?"

"I told you. Roger is not a date." She'd thought she'd explained Roger at the restaurant, but from Grant's behavior, he didn't believe her. Holding back a grin of mischief, she couldn't wait for him to meet her eighty-four-year-old friend. "Trust me on this. Roger will not mind in the least."

Grant gave a little shrug of surrender. "Okay, then. Why don't I fix us something to drink, instead? Then, I'll help you prepare dinner. Your day has been as long as mine."

Warmed by the gesture, she motioned toward the right hand cabinet. "Glasses are on the first shelf, tea and soda in the fridge."

He started around her, but the narrow kitchen avoided little turning space. Her belly bumped his.

She laughed, blushing. "I don't think there's room in here for the four of us."

"We'll manage." Nonplussed, he reached over her head, bringing his delicious warm, male scent to nose level. As soon as he moved toward the refrigerator, Ariana shifted to the end of the counter and called Roger, asking him to come right over. Having Roger around would get her mind off Mr. Perfect.

When her elderly neighbor arrived, sprightly stepping into the apartment with a checkerboard beneath one arm, Ariana watched the expression on Grant's face change from disapproval to amused surprise. Meeting his twinkling gaze, she laughed out loud. So, he *had* thought Roger was a real date.

Following introductions, the three sat down to eat the simple dinner of lasagna, salad and bread. In minutes, Grant and Roger were arguing good-naturedly over who would win the World Series.

At meal's end, Roger pushed back his plate and patted his stomach. "Good dinner, Ariana." Then he reached inside his tan cardigan, pulled out a letter and thrust the white envelope toward her. "I got another one of those notices. Will you take a look?"

Roger suffered with poor eyesight and frequently asked Ariana to read his mail. Ariana perused the letter and frowned, anger rising. "They're threatening a lawsuit unless you pay them $543 for services rendered."

"I don't know what they're talking about. They never rendered any kind of services."

"A lawsuit?" Grant asked, leaning forward with interest. "Mind if I take a look?"

At Roger's nod, Grant took the letter and read it. "This could be a scam. If you'd like, I could look into it on your behalf."

"He's a lawyer," Ariana told Roger reassuringly. "He knows about this kind of thing."

Roger's watery brown eyes widened. An embarrassed flush brightened the paper-thin skin of his cheekbones. "I can't afford a lawyer, either, Ariana. You know that."

Grant waved off his concerns. "I'll take care of it."

The old man stiffened, radiating insult. "Roger Patrinsky pays his own way."

"No wonder you get along so well with Ariana," Grant muttered. "Okay, then. How about a little wager on that checker game? Best two out of three. You win, I have to take care of this matter free of charge. You lose, and you're on your own."

Roger squinted, considering. "You wouldn't lose to a man on purpose would you?"

Wearing his most imposing lawyer expression, Grant replied, "I am an attorney. Attorney's hate to lose."

Ariana's heart did a funny flip-flop as Grant carefully negotiated a way for Roger to retain his pride and still have his problem resolved.

"You got yourself a deal, sonny." Roger cackled

and rubbed his hands together. "Clear the decks, Ariana. I'm about to whup this young fella's britches."

With Grant's help, she cleared the table while Roger set up the checkerboard. Inside the kitchen, she separated the leftover lasagna into three containers, one for her and two for Roger to store in his freezer.

Turning, she found Grant holding a glass toward her. "You didn't finish your milk."

She fisted a hand on one hip. "If you hadn't stolen my coffee—my *decaf* coffee—I wouldn't have drunk that much."

"Milk's good for your babies. Drink." At her mutinous expression, he advanced, bringing the glass closer and closer to her mouth. "Open up."

Ariana's pulse leaped at the image of Grant Lawson touching her lips. She grabbed for the glass and gulped down the inch of milk, then backhanded her mouth like a little kid. "There. Are you happy?"

He studied her for a moment, then smiled. "Very."

Pulse thudding oddly, she watched his long, lean body turn and take the few steps to the dining table where he removed his jacket and hung it on the back of the chair.

Goodness, he was bossy. And thoughtful, and protective, and nice. Very nice.

And he proved just how nice over the next hour as he and Roger battled over the checkerboard.

Grant took the first game much to Roger's chagrin, but Roger came doggedly back and took the second game.

Grant loosened his tie and rolled up his sleeves.

"What's the matter, son?" Roger practically sparkled. "Getting a little hot under the collar?"

Grant gave a mock scowl. "You, my man, are a worthy opponent."

"Dern right I am." Roger set the board up for the final game.

Ariana admired the way Grant treated Roger with respect, as the intelligent equal he was, not as a half-blind old man. In the end, when Grant appeared on the verge of winning, Roger gave a shout of victory and jumped his final four checkers in one swift move.

"There. Now, I guess you'll have to take care of that lawsuit for me."

Grant stared at the board in stunned disbelief, then offered Roger his handshake. "A deal's a deal."

And she never knew for certain if he'd let Roger win on purpose.

Afterward, Grant followed Roger to the door and then down the stairs, arguing good-naturedly about a rematch. How smoothly Grant devised a way to see Roger safely down the stairs without the older man ever noticing. Ariana wished she could be so clever.

"I should go, too, Ariana," Grant said when he returned. "You need your rest." He took his jacket from the back of the chair.

"Thank you for being so kind to Roger."

"Kind? The old codger must have cheated me." Rolling down his sleeves, he then shrugged into the suit coat.

Seeing the imposing, ultraprofessional Grant Lawson outside the office behaving like a normal guy with a big heart did strange things to Ariana's insides. He was the kind of man that made a woman lose her good sense. And if there was thing Ariana could not afford to do, it was to lose what little sense Benjy had left her.

"Did you have something to discuss with me about my case?"

"Oh, right. I was having such a good time, I almost forgot." Jamming his hands into the jacket pockets, he took a deep breath. "I located Benjy. He wasn't too pleased to make my acquaintance."

"Imagine that," she said with mild sarcasm.

"I was wounded by his attitude, let me tell you."

Ariana smiled and pushed the hair back from her face. "What did he say?"

Grant's jaw tightened. "Benjy is not happy about your request for support."

"I didn't expect him to be."

"We may have a fight on our hands."

"Can we handle it?"

He smiled, a wolfish sight that surely spelled trouble for an opponent. "Oh, yes. I can handle your Benjy Walburn."

"Okay, then. What's next?"

"You take care of the twins and yourself. I'll see to Mr. Poodle." With a grin and a wink, he moved to the door. "How about lunch tomorrow?"

Ariana shook her head. As pathetic and weak as it sounded, Grant was becoming her knight in shining armor. Suddenly she needed to keep him at arm's length. "I have to conduct a focus group. I'm not sure what time we'll be finished."

He hesitated, one hand on the doorknob. "Okay. Then I'll see you in the morning and again at five."

"Grant—" she started.

"Until your babies are born, I'll drive you." He waved a finger at her. "No argument. Case closed. See you at eight-thirty."

Ariana watched him go, ignoring the little catch beneath her ribs. The twins wrestling again she supposed. Nothing at all to do with the fact that Grant made her feel so content, so protected—feelings she liked far too much.

Chapter Four

Shortly before noon on Saturday, Ariana stood in the alcove outside Grant's apartment fighting second thoughts. Wanting to surprise him with her gifts, she hadn't called, and now hoped she wasn't intruding. But when Grant had confessed to eating most of his meals out, Ariana hurt for him. The dear man needed her help as badly as she needed to repay his generosity.

Hefting the basket laden with home-cooked food and bright flowers, she rang the doorbell.

In seconds the door opened and Ariana almost dropped the wicker container. Dressed only in flannel lounge pants, Grant was shirtless. The white towel draped around his neck and glistening water droplets on the sprinkle of dark chest hair indicated he'd just stepped out of the shower. Whoa, baby! And she'd thought he looked great in a suit!

Ariana swallowed, suddenly self-conscious. She hitched the basket higher, propping it against the doorjamb to relieve her twinging back. "Hi. Have I caught you at a bad time?"

Looking pleasantly surprised, he immediately reached out and relieved her of the basket.

"Not at all. I just returned from the gym and was thinking of going out for a bite to eat."

Working out at the gym. No wonder he looked so fit. She struggled not to stare at his muscular chest, but how could she look elsewhere when she was so short and he was so tall?

"Come on in." Grant stepped aside, hoisting the basket in question. "What's this?"

"A present. A small thank-you." Ariana followed him into the kitchen. She'd never been inside his condo. As she suspected, the place was perfect. Too perfect. White, detached, austere. Grant's house felt more like an office or a hospital than a home. Ariana glanced around at the empty kitchen. No coffeepot or dirty dishes. No books or plants or knickknacks. Nothing to indicate the personality she was coming to admire. He loved sailing and maritime history, but no evidence of his hobbies decorated the house. Poor man, did he actually live in this sterile environment?

Setting the basket on the bar separating the white living room from the black and white dining room and kitchen, Grant didn't seem to notice her interest in his condo. He was too busy sniffing the air. "Something in this basket smells delicious."

"Mama's recipe. Chicken and plantain. You can't get that in a restaurant." To avoid staring at his chest, Ariana lifted out the casserole dish, a bowl of pineapple and avocado salad and a loaf of bread. She'd cheated on the bread, buying the freshly baked Cuban loaf from a local bakery, but the rest she'd made herself. "If you already have plans, you can put this in your refrigerator. Both the casserole and the bread warm up nicely."

"What, are you crazy? I eat out because I don't like to cook, but if someone else is cooking, I'm in." He rubbed his hands together. "You will join me, of course."

"I'd be delighted. The twins are always hungry." She removed a small potted plant from the same basket glad she'd followed her last minute instinct and brought flowers.

Grant blinked in surprise. "No wonder that thing was so heavy. What else do you have in there?"

"Dessert. Chocolate cake." Smiling at his groan of pleasure, she found a perfect spot on the white tiled countertop to display the bright red mums. The colorful flowers warmed the white, sterile looking room several degrees.

Grant came around her to take white plates from the cabinets. Ariana turned to ask about drinks, then wished she hadn't. His physique proved as interesting from the back as from the front. Finely honed muscles flexed across his shoulders and along his biceps as he reached overhead. His back tapered to a narrow waist, and his pants rode low on slim hips. He really needed to put on a shirt!

She turned back to the table and searched for something to take her mind off these aberrant thoughts. She was pregnant, for goodness sake, though perhaps the hormonal roller coaster could be blamed for her irrational mood swings—among other things.

Grant came along side, handing her the plates. "Do you mind setting things out while I find a shirt?"

"No, go ahead." *Please.*

* * *

Grant took less than a minute to grab a gray Henley and yank the soft shirt over his head. Intrigued that Ariana would go to so much trouble for him, he looked forward to spending another meal with her. He didn't know why exactly, only that he found her charming and natural and wonderfully endearing. Though his social calendar was as full as he wanted it to be, he had never met anyone like Ariana among his circle of friends. She was younger than him by several years so perhaps it was that difference that made her seem so unique.

By the time he returned to the kitchen, she had the table ready. His stomach growled as he caught another whiff of her chicken casserole.

"You really didn't have to do this." But he was glad she had.

"You didn't have to take care of that threatening letter for Roger, either."

So that was the reason for her unexpected visit and the home-cooked food. A twinge of disappointment had him shrugging off the compliment.

"That particular guy won't con anyone else for a long time." Then with the smooth expertise that comes with practice, he shifted the subject. He liked Ariana's neighbor and enjoyed ferreting our scurrilous types who tried to scam the elderly, but didn't want Roger or Ariana thinking they owed him anything. "The flowers look nice. Thank you. This place could use some color."

Ariana's hazel gaze said she was not fooled by his sidestepping, but she let the topic rest and studied the room. "I could help you with that if you'd like. Some bright dish towels, a couple of wall hangings, even some of your sailing photographs would liven things up.''

Her offer of help didn't surprise him. He was beginning to recognize Ariana's need to do for others, as well as her penchant for vivid colors.

''I'm open to a few improvements. To tell you the truth, the condo was decorated when I bought it and I've never bothered to change anything.'' Some of his pleasure drained away at the memory. ''At the time, I didn't care one way or another what the place looked like.''

Grant remembered that time like yesterday, though the sharp pain had long since disappeared. This condo had belonged to him, decorated by his ex-wife to suit her tastes, and he'd had to buy his own home from her as part of the divorce settlement.

''I could get some plants for the balcony, too,'' Ariana was saying. ''Something in autumn colors would look beautiful out there. In fact, I have a huge pot of orange and yellow mums that needs dividing.''

Grant shoved Tiffany and the long ago divorce to the far recesses of his mind. Good mood returning he scooped Ariana's Cuban casserole onto his plate, enchanted by her determined effort to help him. ''Ariana. Please. You've done enough to repay me. Even this meal is too much.''

''I enjoy cooking for my friends.''

So he ranked as one of her friends? The idea appealed to him more every time he saw her. Friendship he could do.

''Well,'' she said, with a sassy tilt of her head. ''Are you going to eat that chicken or admire it?''

''Why? Are you cooking for Roger and the entire senior citizens organization later today?''

"Not tonight. I do that on Monday nights."

His fork froze halfway to his lips. "In your condition? You have to be kidding?"

"I love doing things for other people."

"Yes, I know, but you're pregnant."

"Really? I hadn't noticed."

He laughed, pointed a fork at her, and teased. "All right, woman. I can see, as your attorney, I will have to curtail some of your activities. You shouldn't overdo."

"Is bossing me around part of the attorney-client relationship?"

"Absolutely."

"You'll have to follow me to boss me, but that's okay. We could use an attorney at the halfway house."

His eyebrows arched into his hairline. The woman exhausted him. And herself. She needed a keeper whether she knew it or not. "Another voluntary activity?"

"Mmm-hmm." She pushed the cake toward him. "This one's easy. I do a little PR work so the neighbors accept having these guys in their neighborhood." She grimaced. "That's where I met Benjy."

Figured. Now, he'd make certain she never went there alone again. She was too sympathetic for her own good.

Taking a hefty portion of cake, he started to slice a piece for her when she shook her head. "None for me, thanks." She patted her middle. "Too many calories."

Settling back into his chair, he looked her up and down. He liked doing that and was glad for the excuse. "Your weight doesn't appear to be a problem."

She stared at him, incredulous. "Have you looked at me lately?"

"As a matter of fact, I just did." Not that he wanted her to know he'd been sneaking glances ever since she came in the door. But she looked adorable wearing that denim jumper thing with a bright yellow shirt beneath. The rich color did amazing things to her dark skin. "Your extra weight is all babies. Not an ounce of fat elsewhere."

"I hope you're right. I can't wait to wear my regular clothes and sleep on my stomach again."

An image of her sleeping, dark hair fanned out across the pillow, flashed in his head. He pushed the picture out as quickly as it came.

"Six weeks is not much longer."

"I know. It's actually very soon considering I don't have things ready for the babies. When Benjy took all my savings—"

"He did what!" No wonder she was financially strapped.

"He had an investment opportunity that sounded like a great way to make money for our future, so I gave him the savings." Mouth twisting wryly, her shoulders sagged. "That was three days before the wedding that never happened."

Grant had the strongest urge to inflict violence on Benjy Walburn. And he was not a violent man. "That may qualify as fraud. Do you want to press charges?"

Ariana shook her head, clearly troubled by the idea. "I gave him the money, Grant. He didn't steal it."

The woman was too nice for her own good. "How are you going to manage until I get some sort of settlement from this guy?"

"Oh, don't worry. I know how to pinch pennies and make do. Secondhand stores sell good quality baby items, so I plan to go baby shopping with my next paycheck.'' She dug into the pocket of her denim jumper and extracted a glossy department store ad. ''See this?'' She held the photo of a double stroller out toward him. ''Won't the babies be adorable riding in that? I can push them all over town showing them off.''

''You're going to make a great mother.''

Ariana's face softened with love. ''Before I got pregnant, I never understood the fierce attachment a woman has for her unborn child. I still can't explain it, but now I understand it.''

Ariana was a sweet woman whose caring spirit had cost her a great deal. Seeing how much she loved her unborn children, Grant made a vow. None of them would do without anything they needed as long as he was around. As her attorney, he'd make certain Benjy Walburn did his part to support Ariana and the twins. As a friend, that was the least he could do.

Sitting in his office a week later, Grant remembered his promise when the bad news arrived. He hung up the telephone with an angry thunk.

Every day since she'd arrived on his doorstep with her casserole and flowers, he'd enjoyed Ariana's pleasant laughter and easy company. And for reasons he couldn't quite articulate, he'd taken her to lunch several times, too. Then yesterday, she'd brought the mums over for his balcony, along with some marinated pork that made his mouth water. They'd sat out on the balcony exchanging small talk and laughing at a pair of golfers on the course down below who cheated each other outrageously.

Now, as he frowned at the telephone, a mountain of paperwork piled on his desk, he wondered how Ariana would react to the latest news. Not well, he was certain.

Seated in the chair across from Grant, Brett Hamilton, Wintersoft's vice president of Overseas Operations, leaned forward.

"I say, Lawson, you don't look pleased," Hamilton commented in his understated British way.

Grant tapped a pen hard against the cherry wood desktop. "I have some bad news for a client."

"Not the lovely and expectant Ariana, I hope."

Surprised, Grant scowled at his co-worker. How had Hamilton reached that conclusion so easily?

"Yes. I'm afraid so." He rummaged through a file and pulled out a document. "Would you mind if my assistant looks over this contract for you? She'll be the one doing the research anyway."

"Not at all."

Grant led Brett into Sunny's work area, apprised his paralegal of Hamilton's needs and left them. He could study the information later after Sunny dredged up all the particulars.

With dread clenching his stomach into a knot, he crossed the yellow hardwood corridor toward the public relations department. He tapped softly on Ariana's door, then stepped inside.

"Hi, Grant." Her welcoming smile made him feel worse.

"Can you take a break?"

An appealing furrow appeared between her dark brows. "Not now." She fanned a graceful hand over a cluttered desk that appeared to have exploded in work. "I'm a little overwhelmed today. My assistant is out, and Mr. Winters wanted to look at these media kits by Friday. And I've put off the video for the upcoming trade show as long as I can. I'm swamped."

She was already stressed enough and he had to add to her problems.

Swallowing an inward sigh, he said, "We need to talk. Call me when you have a few minutes." He turned to leave.

"Grant."

Pausing, he took a deep breath, and turned back to where Ariana studied him with concern. Above a lime green dress, her changeable eyes had turned the soft green of elm buds in the spring. "Are you okay?"

Grant's gut twisted. Leave it to Ariana to worry about him first.

"Your ex-fiancé's attorney contacted me."

Tension sprang to her shoulders. She sat up straighter. "Benjy hired an attorney?"

Grant came around her desk to soften the inevitable blow. Might as well tell her straight out. "According to the attorney, Benjy hardly knows you. He's denying paternity and plans to fight support every step of the way."

All the color bleached from Ariana's dark complexion. She wrapped both arms around her middle, instinctively guarding her babies. Sure enough, she was not taking this well.

"I should have expected this." Her voice was as small as a child's. "You tried to warn me that this could happen, but it hurts anyway."

Concern lay like a weight in Grant's chest. Rolling her chair out from the desk, he crouched in front of her and took her hands, rubbing them between his. Her skin was soft, velvety so.

"I'm sorry, angel." The endearment slipped out on its own, but Ariana didn't seem to notice. "Don't be upset. I'll take care of it." He'd almost said I'll take care of you. And he would. He wanted to.

Green eyes luminous with unshed tears, Ariana gazed at him. "I know I'm overreacting, but—" Her lip quivered.

Grant ached with the need to squeeze the life out of her rotten ex. Blast Benjy Walburn and his selfish attempt to strike back at Ariana's rightful request for support.

With valiant effort, she drew in a deep breath, then exhaled in a rush as she pressed both palms to her cheeks and squared her shoulders. "Don't pay me any mind. I'm only being hormonal, but I'm okay."

"No, you're not." But he wanted her to be. Just as he wanted to find a way to crush the cockroach of a man who had the power to hurt her.

"I will be." She forced a quavering smile. "I have the best lawyer in Boston."

Grant's chest constricted. He was her attorney and she trusted him. Taking on the stress was his job. She tried to be brave and strong, but she'd be a mother soon, with two babies demanding constant attention. What she needed was some time away, to forget Benjy and her problems, to relax and rest.

Recalling another, more pleasant telephone conversation today, Grant made a quick decision.

"Ariana." He recaptured her cold fingers, squeezing them reassuringly. "My family has a beach house on Cape Cod. We're all going down this weekend. Come with me."

Always his solace, the beach house provided the perfect opportunity for Ariana to get away. Once there, he had the pressure from his dad to consider, but that was an ongoing problem that didn't involve Ariana.

Surprised, she blinked tear-glossed eyes. "I couldn't impose like that."

"No imposition whatsoever. Mom and Dad love company. My sister, Vanessa, will be there with her husband and daughter—whom you must meet. You'll love Joy. And I've even scheduled perfect weather for you." The joke brought a small smile to Ariana's trembling lips. "Come on. There is no better place to forget your troubles."

"Won't your parents think it odd that you'd bring an overly pregnant woman whom they've never met to their beach house?"

He shook his head. "In the past I've invited a number of clients down. Dad does, too, on occasion." He didn't mention that none of those clients had been female. Now that he'd asked her, Grant warmed to the idea of showing Ariana the beach where he'd spent every summer of his boyhood.

"I'd be a fifth wheel, in the way. You'll want this time with your family."

He raised his palm in a stop sigh. "Objection. Speculation on the part of the witness." At his silliness, Ariana's pretty lips lifted in a full-fledged smile. "You will be my guest and my sidekick."

"Well…"

Regardless of her hesitancy, he could see she was tempted. If Ariana thought she was doing him a favor, she'd jump at the offer. "I haven't had a new person to show off my sailing expertise to in years. I'll be disappointed if you refuse."

Psychological blackmail was a lawyer's dirty trick, but since this was the best thing for Ariana, he didn't feel badly at all when she capitulated under the pressure.

"A weekend at the beach sounds wonderful. Thank you, Grant. You're such a good friend. I'd love to go."

With a gentle clap of his hands he stood, feeling inexplicably chipper as he made his way to the door. "Don't worry about your case. Everything will work out for the best."

As he left her office, taking the vision of her brave little smile with him, he hoped and prayed he was right.

Before the week ended, Emily Winters stopped by Carmella's office to share the latest news on the office grapevine.

"What do you suppose this means?" Emily asked after explaining that Grant had invited Ariana to his family's beach house for the weekend.

"I'm not sure," Carmella answered. "But I know one thing. They've been spending a lot of time together lately."

"Yes, but they could be working on Ariana's custody case."

"Not all the time." Carmella's romantic inclinations came to the fore. "Grant is behaving out of character. He makes several trips a day down the hall to Ariana's office."

"Really?" Emily considered this interesting bit of news.

Eyes dancing, Carmella gave a knowing nod. "And I've watched them in the elevator. He's very gentle, solicitous, almost protective. I'm certain I detect sparks."

A smile bloomed in Emily's chest and spread to her face. "In that case, I suggest we keep our eyes open and see where those sparks lead."

Maybe this time one of their bachelors would find romance without her or Carmella's interference. And that would be a tremendous relief to Emily, and a stroke of luck for everyone concerned.

Chapter Five

"It looks like a postcard," Ariana said in awe, craning her neck from one side to the other to take in the magnificent scenery along Cape Cod.

"What does?" From his place behind the steering wheel, Grant smiled at her.

"That." She pointed to an old rock windmill. "And that." Twisting to the side she motioned to a cottage surrounded by mums and pumpkins and glorious foliage. Her head spun to the right. "And over there. In the distance. Is that a lighthouse?"

A warm, deep chuckle issued from Grant's sweater-clad chest. Casually dressed for the cooler weather, he seemed happier than she'd ever seen him.

"I thought you'd enjoy the Cape."

"I love it. Growing up in Florida put ocean water in my veins, but this is way different from the Gulf."

Since the day she'd agreed to accompany Grant, her nerves had been stretched tighter than her belly button. What would his family think of her? She'd made so many errors in judgment lately that she second-guessed her every decision. She didn't want to cause Grant any embarrassment.

Turning onto a quiet, tree-lined lane, Grant lifted a hand from the steering wheel. "There's the beach house."

Surrounded by a splash of colorful flowers, a lovely two-story Cape Cod Colonial rambled long and wide. Dark blue-gray shutters framed the twelve-pane windows on either side of the oversize brick entryway. In the front yard a pair of maples shed red-gold leaves. The "beach house" was a fabulous home.

Outside a double car garage, a cream-colored Lincoln and a black SUV parked in the driveway.

Ariana's nervous jitters returned. As she suspected, the Lawsons were well-to-do people, not the blue-collar crowd she knew and loved.

"Looks like everyone is here."

Her stomach leaped into her throat.

Grant had been so persuasive, leading her to believe she would receive an open-armed welcome from his family. But now she wasn't so sure. Would they look down upon a doubly pregnant single mother? Would they question Grant's decision to take her case? Would they wonder why on earth he'd brought her into their home?

Head buzzing with misgiving, she accompanied Grant up the cobblestone walk, through the white-columned entry and into the home. The exact opposite of Grant's sterile condo, this place was awash in airy light, warmed by the rich polished wood floors, thick area rugs, and pleasing aroma of spiced tea. Someone in Grant's family knew how to make a house into a home.

"Mom. Dad," Grant called, dropping both his and her luggage in the natural stone entry.

A furry yellow body exploded from behind the stairway to the left and plowed into Grant's legs. A Labrador retriever the size of a sixth-grader groveled and whined at their feet.

"Hello, boy." Going down beside the dog, Grant looked up. "Ariana, meet Buddy, my sister's oldest child."

Ariana bent to pet the friendly, smiling dog. "Hi, Buddy."

"Uncle Gwant. Uncle Gwant!"

The childish voice came from above them. Using the dog as a lever, Ariana straightened in time to see an angelic vision with dark, bouncing curls race down the stairs as fast her short legs could go without tumbling face first to the bottom. The little girl, about three-years-old, she guessed, kept one small hand on the banister while the other waved in excited greeting.

Grant started toward her, but not before she launched off the next-to-the-last step into his arms. The child, apparently, did not find her "Uncle Gwant" at all imposing or reserved as he held her aloft and twirled in a circle. The little girl's squeal of delight mixed with the warm rumble of Grant's laughter. The dog waded in with a round of ear-splitting barks. The ruckus alerted the household and in seconds, four adults joined the melee.

Ariana stood back, hovering in the background as Grant and his family exchanged happy greetings. She missed this kind of gathering with her own rowdy bunch of loved ones. Grant, so distant and businesslike at work, came alive in the company of his family.

When the clamor died down, Grant, holding the little girl in his arms, turned his attention to his guest.

"Everyone, this is the client and co-worker I told you about, Ariana Fitzpatrick. Ariana, meet my parents Royce and Suzanne Lawson, my sister Vanessa and her husband, Patrick Bradford."

Feeling abnormally shy, Ariana shook hands with each one. All the Lawsons were dark-haired, though Royce wore distinguished gray sideburns. While Grant and his father were tall, Suzanne and Vanessa were closer to Ariana's height. And everyone one of them were blue-blood New Englanders to the core.

Ariana warmed immediately to Vanessa and Patrick whose welcomes were as genuine as the dog's. And Grant's effusive, charming father behaved as though he'd known her forever. On the other hand, Suzanne Lawson carried the same reserve that characterized her son. Her smile was tentative at best, her blue eyes searching. Ariana had the feeling she was on probation.

"And this little munchkin," Grant concluded with a finger poke to the child's tummy, "is Joy."

Deep dimples creased round cheeks as the aptly named child beamed at Ariana. "Hewwo. Are you Uncle Gwant's girlfriend?"

"Good heavens no, Joy." Grant's mother cut in. "Uncle Grant is working on a case for Ariana."

"Oh."

It was clear to all that the child had no idea what a case was or that she had made all of them uncomfortable with her innocent faux pas.

From the expression in Suzanne's blue eyes, she worried that the child might be correct. Ariana wanted to tell the woman how wrong she was. Regardless of how much she liked and appreciated him, Ariana was not in the market for a romantic relationship. Hadn't she made enough mistakes in that department to last a lifetime? No matter how handsome and chivalrous Grant might be he was only her attorney and friend.

And even if Ariana were to have designs on Grant, didn't Suzanne know her son better than that? A man such as Grant had so much to offer. Though Ariana's insides pinched to think it, why would he be interested in someone like her?

Moving the conversation to safer ground, Ariana rescued Grant's mother from the awkward moment. "You're home is gorgeous. Thank you for allowing me to intrude on your weekend."

"No intrusion at all, isn't that right, Suzanne?" Royce said. "We're delighted when guests come. A place like this is meant to be shared."

"If you'd like, we'll take you on a tour later after you've settled in," Mrs. Lawson offered. "Some of the house's original elements are breathtaking."

"I'd like that very much." Ariana managed a relieved smile. "Historic homes hold a special fascination for me, and Massachusetts is rich in them. I've spent hours touring the marvelous colonials in Boston."

"Really?" For the first time, Suzanne's cool blue eyes warmed. "Have you seen the Lyman Estate?"

"Not yet, but I've heard it's wonderful."

"Beyond wonderful. The camellia greenhouse alone is worth the trip. Some of those plants are more than a hundred years old."

Bored with the adult conversation, Joy wiggled down from Grant's arms and dashed off with the dog as the adults moved toward the living room.

"Anyone want something to drink? Soda? Coffee? Tea?" Vanessa asked, then glanced at Ariana. "Milk?"

Ariana laughed, liking Vanessa more every minute. She settled into the firmest looking of the overstuffed chairs. "You sound like your brother."

"Lord forbid. He's so stuffy." Vanessa perched on her husband's chair arm and made a face at Grant.

He scowled in return. "Messy Vanessy," he teased. "You only think I'm stuffy because I was never grounded for having three week's supply of dried, crusty food bowls under my bed."

Vanessa fluffed her hair at him. "I'm artistic. What can I say? We creative types can't be bothered with mundane cleaning chores."

"Did your creative type remember her camera?"

"Like American Express, dahling," she teased. "I never leave home without it."

"Vanessa's a professional photographer," Grant said to Ariana in explanation. "A darn good one, too."

"Why thank you, brother. Maybe you aren't so stuffy after all."

Though Grant laughed along with the rest of his family, Ariana noted the pleasure never reached his eyes. Something about the remark bothered him.

"You'll have to pardon my children, Ariana." Royce flashed her a million-dollar smile that would sway any jury. "Sibling rivalry remains alive and well."

"From all the motion going on in here," Ariana lay a hand atop her stomach. "I think my twins have already started."

"Twins!" Vanessa squealed. "Mom, did you hear

that? She's having twins. Isn't that adorable? I wish I would have been a twin.''

From his chair next to his father, Grant uttered a mock groan. ''The world couldn't have stood the strain.''

Suzanne rolled her eyes. ''And neither could my nerves.''

Tension slowly drained out of her shoulders as Ariana joined in the laughter. The rest of the Lawsons appeared every bit as gracious as their son.

Vanessa waved her hand in a shooing motion. ''Why don't you men run along and do something masculine like bring in the luggage or light the grill and let us ladies talk.''

Grant's eyebrows shot up. ''I thought you were getting us something to drink.''

''Later, later, later. Ariana's having twins and that's ever so much more entertaining.''

Patrick, as blond as his wife was dark, spoke up for the first time. ''Come on, men, I know where they stash the soda. We can find our own.''

Vanessa gave him a sugary smile. ''Would you bring us one, too, honey?''

Patrick bent and kissed her on the nose. ''You got it, beautiful.''

Grant shook his head in mock despair. ''Patrick, the woman has you wrapped around her little finger.''

''I know.'' Patrick's besotted smile rested on his wife. ''Isn't she great? Someday the right woman will make you as happy as your sister has made me.''

''Count me out of that dire prediction,'' Grant growled, all humor disappearing.

Patrick only laughed and led the way out of the room, but Grant's reaction disturbed Ariana. He hadn't been joking. Why would Mr. Perfect, a brilliant lawyer who was as gorgeous as sin, be so negative about marriage?

Ariana heard the dog's bark and the tinkling bells of a child's laugh as she followed the narrow, sandy path from the back of the house down to the private beach. Scrub pine and ruby regosa along each side blocked her view except for the occasional sighting of a flying object. Overhead a white Frisbee sailed against the backdrop of blue morning sky.

"Good morning." Grant spotted her the moment she came through the space in the fence. Dark hair tousled in the slight breeze, he looked handsome in a gray ribbed knit pullover above tan khakis.

He turned and came toward her, causing a flutter of attraction. Well, okay, she was pregnant, not dead, and any living female would realize that Grant Lawson was more than handsome. He was a hottie. "Sleep well?"

"Like a baby," she answered with a smile and a downward glance.

In the cool sunshine, Ariana was glad for her own heavy slacks and bright orange sweater, though she likely resembled a pumpkin more than a hottie.

The yellow lab bounded up to Grant, dropped the Frisbee at his feet, and looked up with expectancy on his happy face. Joy tumbled after the dog, giggle as welcome and high-pitched as jingle bells on Christmas Eve.

Grant took the Frisbee and hurled it, sending both dog and child on another merry chase. All along the beachfront, gulls soared and called out in the rhythmic song that heralded mornings on Cape Cod.

"Where is everyone?" Ariana asked.

The house had been strangely silent this morning after last night's noisy cookout, followed by a rousing, but friendly game of canasta. Ariana, who'd been teamed with the ladies against the men, found herself yearning for a similar evening with her own family in Florida. She hadn't been home since last Christmas and unless she got her act together soon, she might miss this Christmas, too, a thought she found singularly depressing.

"Dad and Patrick are down the beach a ways." Grant's blue gaze settled on her face and sent a puzzling shiver through her veins. "Mom and Vanessa went antiquing, so I'm stuck with the munchkin." He didn't sound the least annoyed about that. "They wanted to invite you along, but I wouldn't let them wake you." He turned to watch the toddler and the dog, and when the pair started back toward him, he went on. "You came here to rest, not be dragged all over the Cape looking at old things."

Never mind that the peaceful night's sleep, with the sound of the ocean as her lullaby, had been exactly what she needed, she couldn't allow Grant to coddle her this way. It was—it was—it was too nice, that's what it was!

"I happen to like old things." Brushing back a lock of flying hair, she tucked the strand behind one ear and sent him a chastening scowl.

With a laugh, he threw a hand out to each side. "Which must mean you like me."

"Oh, yeah, like you're an antique."

"Thirty-five is feeling older every day. Seems like only yesterday I was the munchkin's age." He nodded toward his niece, playing along the beach, the watchful Buddy at her side. "She loved playing 'Ring-Around-the Rosy' with you last night."

"The 'all fall down' part was easy. Getting back up proved a bigger challenge."

Chuckling at the image, Grant tapped her on the nose. "I thought you looked cute."

His comment shocked her. "Cute? As in Humpty Dumpty?"

"Uncle Gwant." Face alight, Joy's chubby three-year-old legs plowed through the pale sand. "Look what I finded."

The scent of salt and sea stirred the morning air, and the slight dampness sent Joy's angel curls into fine whorls around her dimpled face.

Grant crouched beside the child, seriously examining the shell. "Look at this, Ariana. Joy's found a clam shell."

Using Grant's shoulder for support, Ariana studied the shell with all due seriousness. Ignoring the strong, heated muscle beneath her fingers, she told the child, "This was once a clam's house."

"It was?" Joy's expression said she couldn't fathom anything living inside so small a place. "Can we look for more? Maybe somebody will still be at home in one of them."

Dusting sand down the legs of his slacks, Grant returned the shell to the child, then stood and exchanged amused glances with Ariana. "Get your pail. We'll see what the tide has brought this morning."

The child trundled up to the fence and returned in seconds, carrying a bright purple plastic bucket. The trio meandered along the shore, seagulls calling overhead, white sails in the distant waters. They chatted idly—recalling funny events from the evening before, commenting on the beautiful autumn and precious little girl, sharing bits of office talk.

Buddy made an occasional foray into the surf, returning to shower the humans with mischievous shakes. Soaking in the sun, the sea, and the company, Ariana felt more positive about her life than she had in a long time. Her gaze slid to the tall, masculine figure strolling beside her. With misgiving, she had to credit Grant for the change, though she was still baffled about why he would go to such lengths for a pregnant, jilted co-worker.

"Here's one, Joy. An oyster, I think." Using the toe of his shoe, Grant poked at a shell buried in the sand. "Wonder how he got here?"

Bucket to one side, the child bent to prod chubby fingers at the bivalve.

Grant crouched next to his niece and picked up the shell.

"Some oysters have pearls inside," he told her, smoothing the sand away for a better look.

Joy squatted with chubby hands atop her thighs, face earnest as she peered from her beloved uncle to her treasure. "A neckwace is in there?"

Shaking his head, Grant said, "Not an entire necklace like Gramma's. Only one single bead."

"Can I see?"

"Sorry, munchkin, but this oyster is at home. We wouldn't want to disturb him."

Baby eyelashes batted innocently. "I just want to say hewwo."

"I know, sweetheart, but oysters aren't like people. If we open his house, he can't close it again."

Her rosebud mouth formed an "o". "Can we take him home wiff us?"

"I'm afraid not. Oysters need the sea like you need the air. He'll die if we take him away from the bay."

A fierce frown creased the adorable face as Joy gave full consideration to this news. "Put him back, Uncle Gwant. I don't want him to be died." Chubby fingers patted the shell. "Bye, Mr. Oyster."

Watching them, Ariana felt a splash somewhere in the center of her heart. Grant Lawson would make a wonderful father, so patient and loving. Someday a very lucky child would call him daddy.

A deep sadness pulled at her. She'd dreamed of giving her children such an attentive, responsible father. Instead she could only promise them a loving mom. Would they feel cheated when they were old enough to understand? Would they miss a man's influence, the one thing she could not provide?

A squeal of laughter chased her dreary thoughts into the October wind. Grant and Joy had ventured too near the ocean in their quest to replace the hapless oyster. Now water lapped at their feet. Joy ran backward, giggling as Buddy cavorted around her, splashing water while keeping his body between hers and the surf. Though his tongue lolled with fun, his eyes were alert and watchful. Instinctively the Lab knew his tiny charge was no match for the sea.

"If you're getting tired," Grant said, coming up beside her with Joy riding piggyback, "there are some lounge chairs along the fence a little ways down."

"I'm not tired, but I would love to sit in the sun for a while. Everything about this place is so gorgeous." She followed behind as Grant galloped toward the chairs, Joy thumping his shoulder and calling, "Giddyup, horsey."

Sitting down, she breathed in a deep draft of fresh air. "I've missed this. Nothing like the smell of the sea."

Letting Joy slither from his back to the ground, Grant eased into the chair beside Ariana, enhancing the morning air with the hint of sandalwood and sea-kissed male.

"I can't wait to be out on the water again. Are you up for sailing tomorrow? Or would a canoe be more your speed?"

"How about a tugboat?" She patted her middle.

"Fat chance." And they both laughed at their silliness.

"Even with this bulk, I think I can be a passable first mate."

Elbow against hers, the warmth of his skin penetrated her sweater. First mate. She'd heard that term a hundred times. Why did it take on a new meaning today?

"I wouldn't want you to take on anything too strenuous."

"Don't worry. I'll be fine. Like you, I'm anxious to feel the water beneath me again."

For all their differences, they shared some commonalties. A passion for the sea. A love of family.

"Good. Sailing it is, then."

Seated in front of them in the sand, Joy poured out her seashells and proceeded to count them. Once she passed ten, the numbers grew exponentially.

"One million, ten-fifty," the child announced. "I like this one best." She brought a shell to Ariana for inspection.

Ariana took the smooth pink shell and regarded it with interest. "You're cute, you know that?"

"Yeth." Standing directly in front of Ariana, her eyes level with the pregnant mound, the child asked, "Why is your tummy so fat?"

Ariana returned the shell. "I have babies in there."

"Babies." A hushed awe filled her voice. "Uncle Gwant. Ariana has babies in her tummy."

"I know, munchkin. Two of them." Rising with athletic grace, he retrieved the Frisbee and tossed it for the dog.

Joy moved closer, eyes pinned to Ariana's belly. "Can I see them?"

Ariana laughed. "Not yet."

"If we open their house will they die like Mr. Oyster?"

"Something like that." At the child's disappointed expression, Ariana quickly added, "But you can feel them."

"I can?" Hope lit the cherubic face.

Ariana took the toddler's hand and lay the tiny fingers on her stomach. "You may have to wait a minute, but—" The twins performed on cue. "There. Do you feel that?"

Joy answered by placing her other hand next to the first. "Do it again."

Ariana laughed again, catching Grant's indulgent, adoring glance. She felt undeniably happy to be on this beach with this child and that man.

"Uncle Gwant, come here. Hurry. Feel Ariana's babies."

A warm flush of embarrassment, mixed with a longing she didn't understand, flooded Ariana. Feeling Grant's eyes on her, she lowered her head. Her pulse thudded strangely, and rigor mortis seemed to have settled into her limbs.

"Uncle Gwant, hurry. Come on. Right here." Patting Ariana's tummy, the child grew insistent.

Grant cleared his throat. An electrical charge hung

in the air as Ariana searched for a graceful way to free Grant from doing such an intimate thing if he didn't want to.

But what if he wants to?

The thought danced on the fringes of her mind, like an imp sent to torture her, while the request hung in the ocean air.

To break the spell, Ariana pulled the child to her side and hugged her. She smelled of saltwater and roses with a hint of Buddy, the Lab, tossed into the mix.

Would her own children smell and feel so delightful? Would they be as precocious and guileless as Joy? Would they have a role model in their lives as fine as Grant?

The thought drew her gaze back to him. Standing with both hands in his pockets, black hair tossed by the breeze, he stared out at the lapping waves, his profile serious, almost pensive. Had Joy's childish request upset him? She didn't know whether to apologize or let the matter go. She chose the latter.

"Grant."

He turned to look at her, eyes hooded.

Ariana raised her palms. "This fat lady could use a hand up."

His shoulders relaxed. The corners of his mouth tipped up and the electric charge dissipated. The moment passed, but the idea had been planted, and Ariana couldn't get the thought out of her mind. What would it be like to have Grant put his long, elegant hands against her body and share the wonder of her unborn babies? With a shock, she realized she'd wanted him to. Yet, he'd turned his back, uncomfortable with the thought of touching her, clearly repelled by her overly pregnant body. She didn't know why that hurt. It shouldn't have. But it did.

Chapter Six

The scent of mulled cider and the soft drift of voices drew Ariana out of her guest room and toward the staircase. Halfway down, she heard her own name and froze, one hand gripping the banister.

"Ariana is a lovely person, don't you think, Mom?" Ariana recognized the voice as Vanessa's. She and Mrs. Lawson must be in the living room situated behind and to the right of the staircase.

"She seems to be."

"I think Grant is interested in her."

"As a client, yes." Suzanne drew the words out thoughtfully. Ariana could almost visualize the pucker between her brows. "Grant's brought many clients here over the years."

"All of whom were male that did nothing but talk shop and play golf, no personal conversations whatsoever. I've learned more about Ariana this weekend than I ever knew about Tiffany."

Surprise filtered over Ariana. Grant told her that he

brought clients here, but he hadn't mentioned that she was the first female. Tightening her hold on the banister, she leaned forward.

"I think you're reading more into this than exists," Suzanne was saying.

"She makes him laugh, Mom. When was the last time you saw Grant this relaxed and happy? Did you see his expression when she told that story about the fish pulling her overboard on one of her dad's fishing excursions? He was enchanted, charmed. I think he's falling for her."

"Don't be ridiculous." Suzanne's voice was sharp as the spines on a sea urchin. "Grant has a compassionate side. He's only trying to help her out of the awful situation she's gotten into."

Ariana hugged her midsection. While immensely disappointed that she'd been unable to make her relationship with Benjy work—or to succeed at any relationship for that matter—she was nonetheless ecstatic to have these babies. She would not let her children think they were an "awful situation".

Vanessa's voice drifted up to her again over the rattle of cup against saucer. "Mom, if you can't see the way Grant watches her, you aren't looking."

Ariana's mouth went dry. Grant watched her? She glanced quickly around as if expecting to find him lurking in the shadows with a pair of binoculars.

"Grant is her attorney, Vanessa, and you know how seriously he takes his work. He feels responsible for her until she has a settlement from that fiancé of hers."

Vanessa laughed. "Okay, have it your way, but I for one would be glad to see Grant put Tiffany behind him and find some happiness. My brother is a great guy who deserves more than he's settled for since she divorced him. He's locked his emotions away too long and that can't be healthy."

"I won't argue that. His business-only lifestyle worries me."

"Then stop putting up roadblocks. For the first time in three years he's showing interest in a bright, lovely woman that I happen to like very much."

Suzanne's long-suffering sigh could be heard all the way up the stairs. "I want him to be happy, but I'm not sure Ariana…"

Ariana had heard enough. Too much, actually. Mama was right. Eavesdroppers never hear anything good about themselves.

Surely Vanessa was mistaken. Grant wasn't interested in her. And other than the rich friendship growing between them, she wasn't interested in him. Not in that way. With chagrin, she thought back to those moments on the beach when she'd longed to take their friendship one step further.

Ariana battled dismay. Hadn't she learned one thing from her disastrous romantic entanglements?

Friends didn't let you down. Lovers did.

As quietly as possible, she hastened back up to the guest suite, head throbbing in consternation.

When she returned sometime later, Suzanne and Vanessa sat side by side on the sofa, a stack of photo albums on the coffee table in front of them.

Vanessa glanced up, saw Ariana and smiled. "Hi. Enjoy your nap?"

"I don't know what's gotten into me lately. I could sleep forever." The fact that her nap was over thirty minutes ago didn't matter.

"Your body's gearing up for the big event. I think

I slept the first three months *and* the last three months of my pregnancy, didn't I, Mom?''

Suzanne gave an affectionate nod. ''Poor Patrick. He thought she was in a coma those last two weeks.''

Vanessa scooted to one side, making room on the sofa. ''Join us, Ariana. We're reminiscing over old pictures while the guys are off chasing a golf ball and the baby is napping.''

Ariana took the open space beside Vanessa, peering with interest at the photo albums. Over the next half hour, she learned about Grant's childhood from the photos of his summers on Cape Cod and the stories his mother and sister told.

''That's Grant and me,'' Vanessa said at length. ''See? Grant has a black eye where I bopped him with a toy truck.'' She tapped a long fingernail against the smiling faces of two young children playing in the water. The boy, did indeed, sport a black eye. ''How old were we, Mom?''

''That was the year Grant turned seven and you were not much older than Joy. You cried longer over that black eye than he did.''

''I remember that! Grant felt terrible because I was so upset. His eye was swollen shut, but he kept trying to comfort me.''

''That's because you wouldn't shut up and I was tired of hearing you cry.'' Grant lounged in the doorway, mouth tilted in a wry grin. ''What are we doing? Boring Ariana with the family history?''

At the sudden unexpected intrusion of Grant's voice, Ariana's breath caught in her throat. She swallowed back the unwanted response, carefully aligning the new information about Grant with his treatment of her over the past few weeks.

Even as a child, Grant's concern had been for others. No wonder he found her case worthy of attention. He was born a soft touch. His concern had nothing to do with her and everything to do with the kind of person he had always been. For some reason, the truth depressed her.

"Yes, brother dear," Vanessa replied with false sweetness. "We've even shown her the one of you on the bearskin rug."

"I think that's you on that rug, sister dear."

"Mother!" Vanessa cried in mock fury. "He's picking on me."

"You started this one, Vanessa," Suzanne replied. "Don't run to Mommy for help."

Ariana enjoyed the affectionate teasing between the brother and sister. Once again, she missed her own siblings and longed to see them. Soon, very soon, she'd have her life under control again so she could take Grant's advice and invite them to visit. She hoped.

Grant came into the room then and settled on the sofa arm beside Ariana. He brought with him the smell of the fresh outdoors mixed with his own unique scent. Pulse strumming in the oddest way, Ariana focused her attention on the photo album.

Vanessa turned the page to a progression of Lawsons over the last twenty-five years. One photo of Grant at about fifteen caught Ariana's eye. Standing on a sailboat wearing that heart-stopping smile, he showed all the potential of the man he would grow to be.

"I remember that day like yesterday." Grant leaned forward. His shoulder brushed Ariana's and his cheek was only inches away. She resisted the crazy urge to stroke her fingers over his strong jawline.

"That was my first time to sail alone." Grant's baritone rumbled next to her ear. "And I was on top of the world."

"How did you do?" Ariana turned, bringing her face so close to his, she could see the tiny laugh lines around his mouth. "Really well, I'll bet."

Blue eyes smiled into hers and Ariana felt the rest of the world fade away until she and Grant were the only two people in the room. With great discipline, she instructed her eyes not to stare at his lips and fought down an almost overpowering need to touch him.

What in the world was happening to her? Was Vanessa's suggestion that Grant thought of her as more than a client playing tricks with her mind?

"Dad let me take her out again the next day, so I must have done fairly well."

"You were a natural sailor." Suzanne's clipped voice defused the moment and Ariana turned back to the album where Grant's mother pointed to more pictures of Grant and his sailboats. "Your father recognized that early on just as we always knew Vanessa had a gift for photography."

"Did you take some of these pictures?" Ariana said to Vanessa, relieved to focus on anything except Grant's nearness. "Grant says you're very good."

Vanessa reached across the protrusion of Ariana's stomach and patted her brother's knee. "Thanks, Grant."

"I only stated the truth." He returned the pat and rose. "I'm famished. Anyone care for a sandwich?"

The women agreed that a sandwich sounded good. Needing to be useful, Ariana struggled upward.

"Let me help you with those." Everyone had treated her as a guest long enough.

Grant pointed a finger at her. "You stay put."

She might have known he wouldn't let her do a thing.

"Bossy." Wrinkling her nose at him, she eased obediently back onto the sofa. Grant sauntered out of the room, one side of his mouth kicked up in a grin.

Ariana forced her attention back to the photos. She knew how he looked from the back. Too darn good. And considering the pointed glances Suzanne and Vanessa exchanged, Ariana couldn't afford to do anything else to cause speculation.

"So," Ariana said, blaming her breathlessness on the two babies pressed beneath her lungs. "Show me some of your photographs."

Vanessa gave her a funny look, glanced once toward the kitchen, then said, "All the rest of the photos in this album are mine, I think."

The quality of the photography had suddenly gone from casual family photos to professional artistry. Ever since her arrival at Cape Cod, Vanessa had been snapping photos, but Ariana had no idea she was so talented.

"Whoa. You *are* good." Ariana gazed down at a younger Grant in cap and gown, surrounded by family, a diploma in one hand. "The emotion is almost palpable."

"That's what I strive for. I don't want to take pictures…I want to capture emotion. Look at Dad's face. What do you see?"

Ariana studied the elder Lawson, knowing Vanessa expected her to find something specific. At last she said, "This sounds crazy, but even though he's smiling, he looks disappointed."

"That's it!" Vanessa crowed. "He *was* disappointed and was trying very hard not to show it, but the camera caught his mood anyway. Grant had announced that he wouldn't be joining the family law firm."

"Royce was devastated," Suzanne put in. "But now, with Royce's retirement only a few years away, he and Grant are currently renegotiating that proposition—much to Royce's delight."

This was news to Ariana who didn't like the idea one little bit of Grant leaving Wintersoft.

"If he's considering the move now, why didn't Grant want to work with his dad's firm from the beginning?" Most young attorneys would jump at the opportunity to join a successful, high-profile firm like Royce Lawson's. Even though the firm was based in Connecticut, they frequently made the news in Boston.

The mother and daughter exchanged glances. In answer, they turned the page and pointed to a photo. A stunning blonde in a silver beaded gown stood next to Grant in front of an enormous, beautifully appointed Christmas tree. Tall and model-thin, she looked like an ad for Miss Universe.

"What a beautiful woman," Ariana murmured, mesmerized as much by the expression on Grant's face as by the blonde.

Vanessa glanced toward the kitchen, then spoke in low tones. "That's Tiffany. Grant's ex-wife. They met when he was in law school at Harvard."

With a sinking sensation, Ariana recognized the caution in Vanessa. Apparently Tiffany was still an unpleasant reminder for Grant.

"Is she the reason he didn't go into practice with your father?"

"At least in part. Tiffany's from Boston and wanted to stay there with her social set. Grant agreed to anything she asked."

Suzanne shook her head sadly. "Look at them. They were so perfect together. I never understood why Tiffany divorced him."

Inadequacy swarmed Ariana. How could Vanessa ever imagine Grant would be interested in short, fat, and dark, when he'd been married to tall, thin, and radiantly blond?

The perfect wife had divorced him. No wonder Vanessa worried about his solitary lifestyle. He was still in love with the beautiful Tiffany.

Given this new information, Ariana carefully shelved the annoying attraction that had buzzed in her veins. Neither she nor Grant were looking for love, but they could both use a best friend. The fact that her conclusion lacked a certain conviction and her stomach felt as heavy as lead didn't matter in the least.

Crouching before the fireplace, Grant lay the logs for a fire they would all welcome later tonight after the sun was gone. From the kitchen came the smells of cinnamon rolls and the sounds of female chatter. He found himself straining for a soft, Florida drawl amidst the clip of New England voices.

His thoughts lingered on Ariana, heavy with child, and the almost overpowering desire he'd endured yesterday on the beach when Joy had urged him to feel the movement of Ariana's twins. He'd experienced a twinge of jealousy, not *of* them, but *for* them, brought on, most likely, by his childless state. That, and watching Ariana struggle to do what was best for her babies, had stirred his latent paternal instincts.

Her laugh, as warm and smoky as campfire, drifted in from the kitchen along with his sister's. Those two got along famously, and the rest of the family liked her, too, though Mom was her usual cautious self.

Affection for his mother expanding his chest, he finished laying the fire and stood, dusting his hands against his pants legs. Whether he was ten or thirty-five, Mom didn't want her baby boy wounded again.

Not that she need fret in that department. After Tiffany's infidelity, he'd vowed never to take another chance on love and marriage. As much as he'd wanted a family, he'd take his fulfillment from the one he had and dote on his niece instead of kids of his own. Tiffany had refused to have children. *His* children, anyway.

Moving to the bookshelves beside the fireplace, he thumbed through a couple of books. Ariana was nothing like Tiffany, though. Kind, and too considerate for her own good, Ariana would never do to a man what Tiffany had done to him.

Ruefully he shoved the novel back onto the shelf and took out another. He'd once believed the same things about Tiffany and look what happened with that. Ariana was pregnant, and even though tests would eventually prove if Benjy was the father, he very well might not be. As much as he despised thinking such a thing, the attorney in him faced the fact. Ariana's unfaithfulness could be the reason Benjy was resisting child support.

As though his thoughts had conjured her up Ariana appeared in the arched opening holding Joy's hand. Vanessa followed behind, chattering away about sunsets and perfect lighting.

Grant's pulse quickened. He refused to consider the meaning as he contemplated his client, searching for deceit.

She looked incredible. Thick brown hair wiggled loose from a charming top-knot. Delicate face scrubbed clean, she'd changed into a heavy blue sweater over blue jeans and looked all of sixteen. His stomach took a dive. Ariana appeared as sweet and guileless as the child holding her hand.

"The sunset is glorious," Vanessa was saying as she grabbed her camera from a small end table. "We're going out to take pictures. Want to come?"

Not usually given to flights of imagination, Grant attempted to shelve his disturbing doubts along with the book in his hand. He'd had no suspicions about Ariana before. Why had they suddenly sprung out of nowhere to torment him?

With great discipline, he contributed the doubts to reminders of Tiffany and struggled not to paint Ariana with the same shade of ruthless dishonesty he'd found in his ex-wife.

"Grant, are you going with us?" his sister demanded, creative juices all but dripping out of her. Before he could answer, Vanessa scooped Joy into her arms and yelled toward the second floor. "Patrick! Hurry, honey. The lighting is perfect."

The doting Patrick pounded down the stairs with a child's jacket in hand. Buddy, the Lab, clambered along behind.

Ariana flashed a smile in Grant's direction. Some of his inner darkness fled.

"Are you too tired for another trek around the beach?" he asked, wanting to walk with her and to dispel the awful discontent that rose within.

"Absolutely not. I'm always rejuvenated after my nap."

When they'd returned from the sailing trip this afternoon, shadows made half circles beneath her eyes, and she'd gone right up to lie down. "Sorry if the sailing trip wore you out."

"I haven't had so much fun or worked so hard on a boat since I was in college. You're a good sailor."

"You're a pretty good first mate, too."

"For a fat, pregnant woman?"

He let his gaze slide over her. "Pregnant, definitely. Fat, hardly."

"Right answer, counselor. No wonder you're such a great negotiator for Wintersoft." She plunked a palm in his direction, nose crinkling merrily. "Come on. Can't miss that sunset."

With an inexplicable leap of anticipation, he took her hand and followed the family out into the Cape Cod evening.

The sunset was, indeed, magnificent, and Vanessa rushed around the beach, snapping shots, ordering various members of the party to stand here or do this, her eye for detail capturing the sun and sea and season to perfection. But when she moved farther down the beach, Grant shook his head. Whether Ariana admitted it or not, she had to be tired.

"You guys go ahead. We'll enjoy the sunset from here. Ariana needs to conserve her energy."

For once, Ariana didn't argue or accuse him of bossiness. They fell in step and he held on to her hand, swinging it between them like kids. The setting sun cast a golden glow over the sloshing surf. Joy's giggle and Buddy's occasional yip carried back to them even when the little family disappeared from sight.

"What does she do with all these pictures?"

"You'd be surprised at her clients. Magazines. Tourism Departments. She travels around New England to festivals, boat races, all the big events, and gets paid great money for the photos she takes.''

''Gee, what a tough job.''

''No kidding. Why couldn't I have been the one in the family with that talent?''

''Your talent lies in another area, counselor, one that I'm particularly grateful for.'' She squeezed his hand lightly.

Pleased, he tried for a nonchalant shrug. ''Law has its rewards.''

''And you are very good at it. I hear you're thinking of joining your father's firm.'' She stopped strolling and dropped his hand, turning to face him.

''Where'd you hear that?''

''Your mother.''

He bent and gathered several pebbles shifting them back and forth between hands. ''Dad is using all his considerable powers of persuasion to make that happen.''

Her beautiful eyes studied him. ''Do I hear a but in there somewhere?''

''You've met my dad. He's flamboyant, charming, and so full of unleashed energy he'd give the Energizer-Bunny a run for his money.'' Heaving a sigh and fighting the inevitable sense of inadequacy that swamped him every time the subject arose, he said, ''My father is the best attorney I've ever known—bar none. He's won more high-profile court cases than anyone in New England and has been courted as a political candidate for years.''

''I see.'' The waning sunlight bathed her skin in gold. ''That kind of reputation is hard to live up to.''

Grateful for her understanding, he agreed. ''Very.''

"But you could. You have the talent, the smarts, the drive."

Her steadfast belief in him soothed away bits of the inadequacy. "I'm good at what I do, Ariana, but I'm not my father."

"And why should you be? You're you."

Drawing back, he tossed one pebble far out in the surf. "That's exactly the problem. Our styles are completely different. Dad relishes the limelight whether he's in front of the news media or a jury. I'm a team player who prefers to stay in the background, to research and negotiate."

He didn't add the rest of his concerns; that he could never live up to his father's expectations, that somehow Dad would be disappointed that he'd hired him on.

"So, are you going to join his firm or not?"

"I told him I'd think about it."

"Do you want to?"

"No."

Ariana shot him a curious frown but didn't say the obvious. If he didn't want to practice his father's kind of law, why would he have to think about it?

Frustrated, he sailed another rock, sent the rounded stone skidding across the tops of gently capping waves. Shadows formed over the water and all around them.

Ariana lay a hand on his arm. "You'll make the right decision. You always do."

Her simple words of reassurance, and her unfounded belief in his ability to do the correct thing, moved him. He resisted the strongest urge to pull her into his arms. Instead he chunked another rock into the sea.

"Let me try that."

Taking a pebble from his outstretched hand, she gave

it a fling. It plopped less than six feet out. "There goes my career with the Red Sox."

"Ah, you're just out of shape." As soon as the words were out, he laughed. "I didn't mean that."

"Yes, you did, and you're right." Arching her back Ariana pushed her stomach forward. "I am seriously out of shape."

She giggled, a light musical sound that swept along his nerve endings like a symphony, easing the pressure from his father.

Suddenly she stilled as if listening to a sound no one else could hear. Her hands went to her midsection, and a look of fascination swept her dark and lovely face.

"The twins?" he asked, knowing full well nothing else could cause that look. He moved to her side, the memory of yesterday morning as fresh as the salt air. He'd wanted to share in the phenomenon then, and now, shrouded in the intimate privacy of twilight, he wanted to even more.

"Yes. They're playful all of a sudden." She turned to face him, belly nearly brushing his. "I think they're laughing at their mother's pitching arm."

Her whimsical outlook did nothing to eradicate his yearning. He didn't know why he suddenly felt so close to her. Maybe because she'd accepted his ambivalence about his father, something he'd never shared with anyone.

He moved closer, sorely tempted. Would he be overstepping the borders of their relationship—whatever that might be? "Ariana…"

His gaze drifted down to where her hands rested, then back up to her changeable eyes. In the fading golden light, they glowed a luminescent green.

Before he could talk himself out of it, he placed a

hand on either side of her belly and drew her to him. He'd expected to be embarrassed or at the least uncomfortable, but he wasn't. He was relieved, as though he'd finally made some sort of a decision.

"You have a miracle in there," his voice was surprisingly hushed, reverent.

"Two of them." She responded in the same hushed tone.

The last faint rays of sunlight disappeared, dropping into the whispering ocean as soundlessly and graceful as a pearl diver.

"Yesterday I thought—" She hesitated.

"You thought what?" Why was he still whispering?

"You didn't seem interested in the babies' movements."

"It's all I've thought about since then." Perhaps not all, but he couldn't yet articulate the others anymore than he could admit wondering about her fidelity, her honesty. He knew she resorted to fibs when backed into a corner. Did her white lies extend to more devious deeds?

The babies moved beneath his touch, and Grant closed his eyes, letting go of doubts, savoring the encounter. This moment in time was all that mattered. The rush of ocean waves against the shore and the scent of salty sea cocooned them in the encroaching darkness like a deep, luxurious dream. When Ariana's small soft hands, cool from the night air, closed over his, he felt the effect all the way to his bone marrow. For a fleeting moment, a time so brief he'd deny it to himself later, he embraced the fantasy that these children belonged to him, and so did their mother. Fiercely, he wanted to protect them from the ugliness in the world.

Ariana needed him. Other than at work, no one had ever needed him. Not his wonderfully adequate, self-sustaining family. Certainly not his ex-wife. But Ariana was alone, a gentle, fragile butterfly, beating her valiant wings against a hurricane.

They stood there, connected in a most elemental way, and Grant's urge to share in her babies shifted and changed. Deep inside, a rusty door creaked open, exposing a raw, empty place he'd kept hidden for years. He had the most frightening need to pull her closer, to lay his mouth over hers, to feel her heartbeat against his.

Their glances connected. Her eyes, green moments ago, now glistened gold in the waning light. She knew. He could read the answering need in those changeable eyes. She knew he wanted to kiss her and she wanted it, too.

He'd allowed their relationship to move rapidly from client to friendship status, but now the boundaries of that relationship had expanded.

A vision of Tiffany rose to mock him. He'd long since stopped loving her, but he'd never forget the treachery a beautiful woman was capable of. Ariana Fitzpatrick, pregnant or not, was exquisite. Different certainly from Tiffany's blond sophistication, but a dark and delicate beauty just the same who caused him to feel things he didn't want to feel and to think things he had no business thinking.

With the great discipline he'd cultivated over the years, he removed his hands and stepped away.

Eyes closed, head cushioned by the leather headrest Ariana stifled a yawn. The predawn trip back to Boston depressed her.

Something sweet and lovely had passed between her and Grant on the beach last night. For a fleeting moment, she'd actually thought he wanted to kiss her. Foolish notion, she knew, and most likely brought on by the intimacy of darkness and the fact that he'd felt the twins move. That in itself was a stirring event that had surprised her no end. Who would have thought that Mr. Perfect would be interested in the quickening of her unborn children?

Rubbing a hand across her belly, she fretted. In the space of only a few short weeks, Grant Lawson had become important to her. Other than her father, he was the most generous man she'd ever known. But kindness didn't cause the sudden lift of her stomach and the stir of excitement when he came into the room.

Disgusted with herself for even going there, she faced the truth she'd battled all weekend. She was more than attracted to Mr. Perfect. Pregnant, fat, totally screwed-up Ariana Fitzpatrick who wouldn't know a decent man if he fell from Heaven, liked her pro-bono attorney a little too much.

Now that she'd faced the truth, she felt better. After all, being attracted to a man was a normal physiological function, even for a pregnant Volkswagen. She could simply put these silly emotions out of her mind and go on as before. They would disappear once she'd won child support from Benjy, and she and Grant were no longer working so closely together.

Satisfied she'd made the right decision, she settled deeper into the seat, stretching her jean-clad legs as far out as possible.

''Are you uncomfortable?''

She should have known Grant would notice the wiggles. Without opening her eyes she muttered, "There should be a law against waking before sunrise."

"I'll take that up at the very next session of the Supreme Court." His voice held amusement.

Ariana peeked out of the corner of one eye, her insides doing a stupid little stutter step. How did he do that? He looked as though he'd been cut out of *GQ* and pasted into the Lexus. She, on the other hand, felt like something scraped from the bottom of a kid's tennis shoe.

"You don't suppose we could find someplace open for coffee, do you?"

"We're the only two conscious people in the universe."

"I was afraid you'd say that. Go ahead. Shove me out, then run over me. I feel like roadkill anyway."

He laughed. "You don't look anything like a dead opossum to me."

"Thanks." She peeked at him again, this time a half grin on her face. "I think."

Grant did have a way of cheering her up.

"Not a morning person, huh?"

"Oh, yes. I'm a morning person." She pointed toward the hovering darkness. "I'm just not a middle of the night person."

"What do you plan to do when the twins come? I suspect they'll like the midnight hours best of all."

"Brats."

He laughed again. "Don't disparage them like that. You'll damage their inner child."

"How can I damage the inner child of an inner child who is not yet an outer child?"

"Ariana, reach behind the seat. Mom sent a thermos of decaf just for you. Drink all of it."

Ariana dove for the hot drink, pouring carefully in deference to Grant's vehicle. After several sips of the fresh ground brew, she sighed. "Your mother is the best. The rest of your family is pretty terrific, too."

"I like to think so."

She sat up straighter to peer out the windshield. The promise of morning shimmered in the sky.

"Vanessa offered to photograph the twins."

"You should let her."

"I will, but not without pay, so I'm doing some PR work for her business in exchange. Being in the debt of one Lawson is bad enough."

"Hey!" He pretended insult. "What's so terrible about me?"

"You're bossy, for one thing." But her mischievous grin gentled the jibe.

"So is my sister. Just wait. She'll not only get that PR work out of you, she'll convince you to let her sell the twins' pictures to some baby magazine."

"She already has."

"Told ya." He cast her another smile. "You seem to be coming alive now."

"The sun is rising." She toasted the eastern sky with her cup. "Only vampires like the dark."

"So, you had a good time this weekend?"

The depression returned, heavy as a wet woolen blanket. "Yes."

"Don't be so enthusiastic. The excitement could cause preterm labor."

"Grant." Cradling the plastic coffee cup, she shifted around in the seat. He glanced at her once, twice, waiting for her to go on. "What happened last night?"

Startled, he turned back to the road. Face in profile, he swallowed. "I'm not sure I know what you mean."

"On the beach."

"Oh." Gaze pinned to the windshield he pulled the old lawyer's trick of answering with a question. "What did you think happened?"

She longed to confess the truth that last night had meant something special. But like those other times when the stakes had been particularly high, she couldn't find the courage, settling instead for the less disturbing white lie. Considering the mistakes she'd made lately, maybe she'd misinterpreted the entire incident.

"Nothing, I suppose. Other than a pleasant walk in the sunset."

"My thoughts exactly." His grip relaxed on the steering wheel, telling Ariana more than his words. The reminder of that sweet moment last night embarrassed him, and he regretted his impulsive behavior.

The knowledge did not cheer her. Returning to her coffee, she let the now visible profusion of color and beauty rush past. With sun breaking through the mists and glimmering on the dew, the October morning was a feast for the senses, and Ariana concentrated on the scenery, refusing to let depression ruin what had been a beautiful weekend.

As they entered Boston and headed toward Wintersoft, Inc., Grant said, "You've grown awfully quiet. Is it something I said?"

"No, no, of course not." It wasn't what he said. It was what he didn't say.

"What's wrong then?"

"Not a thing." Other than being pregnant, unwed, broke, confused and terrified she was falling for her attorney, what could be wrong? "Well, a little tired, perhaps."

A look of misgiving swept over Grant. "Was the trip too much? I wouldn't have encouraged you to go if I'd thought you would overdo."

Now he was sorry he'd taken her.

"The weekend was marvelous. Tired means tired of carrying this VW Beetle around." She balanced the cup atop her belly.

"When do you see your doctor again?"

"Tomorrow." At his raised eyebrow, she finished. "I have less than a month before Hansel and Gretel make their first personal appearance, and since we're dealing with twins, I'll be seeing my obstetrician twice a week from here on out. Maybe more."

A furrow appeared on his handsome brow. "Does that mean something's wrong?"

She shook her head. "We're still on target for a mid-November delivery. Everything about my pregnancy has been perfect from the get-go. Absolutely perfect."

Chapter Seven

A dozen women, all of whom had also swallowed Volkswagens, lined the waiting room the following morning as Ariana left the obstetrician's office and headed toward Wintersoft, Inc. After a delightful weekend with Grant and his family, she'd come back to Boston to a mountain of work, a crisis at the halfway house, a mind full of confused misgivings and now this.

A chill wind whipped in off the ocean, zipping around corners and up dresses. The twins wrestled in protest. Wishing she'd worn a heavier jacket, Ariana boarded the T toward downtown. By the time she reached the concrete and glass building on Milk Street that housed Wintersoft, the muscles in the back of her neck spasmed with tension.

Every fiber of her being wanted to call her mother in Florida and cry on that soft, nurturing Cuban shoulder, but she resisted the urge. Mama had enough worries on her mind. When the time came, Ariana wanted to present herself as a together, stable, single parent capable of caring for herself and her twins. As of today, she was less together than ever.

Finding Lloyd Winters out for the day, Ariana stopped at Emily's office to explain the situation.

The boss's daughter's smile was warm beneath sapphire eyes. "Everything going all right?"

Ariana exhaled loudly. "Actually, no."

Emily's face registered concern. She pushed away from the computer screen. "What's wrong?"

Ariana handed her the doctor's order that had thrown her already topsy-turvy life into total chaos.

"I have to take my leave of absence now. The babies may be in danger."

Grant got the news at four o'clock that afternoon. Fear and anger rippled through him. Fear for Ariana and her twins. Anger because she hadn't told him herself. On the heels of both emotions came an overwhelming sense of responsibility.

He grabbed his coat, shrugging into the garment as he rushed passed Sunny's desk without so much as telling her he was leaving.

The Cape Cod trip was a mistake. She'd overdone. Though he'd been certain the weekend would do wonders for her stress, he'd been wrong. His know-it-all attitude had harmed Ariana and her twins. Tiffany was right. He'd be a terrible father.

By the time he reached Ariana's apartment building, he was a wreck, full of self-recriminations. He bounded up the staircase to the third floor and cursed because he didn't have a key. She was probably in bed, resting, and he'd have to disturb her. Sick and frightened, she would have to struggle out of the bed and stumble to the door. The thought almost made him turn around. Almost. But he was a man who took responsibility seriously. This was his fault and he would take care of the matter.

Startling her would not be a good thing. Rapping softly, he pressed his face close to the door and called. "Ariana."

In seconds, the door popped open. "Grant."

A surprised Ariana stood there, holding a dish towel in one hand, a spatula in the other, and looking pretty darned good in an oversize hot-pink shirt and black, skinny-legged pants. He shoved his way inside.

"Why aren't you in bed?" he growled.

"I'm fixing dinner. Today is Roger's—"

"No, you're not." Amazing smells already emanated from the kitchen. Smells that made him angry. She had no business cooking. "You're going to bed and I'm fixing dinner."

"Grant! This is Roger's birthday. He's eighty-five."

"I don't care if he's the two-thousand-year-old man. You're supposed to be in bed."

Pouting, she reluctantly let him guide her toward the couch. "How do you know that?"

He lifted her feet and shoved two couch pillows beneath them. "Emily Winters told me. Quite by accident, I must admit. She assumed I already knew, given that we'd spent the weekend together." His accusing glare didn't phase her in the least. He *should* have known, and Ariana should have been the one to tell him. "Now, what are we cooking?"

Jockeying for a comfortable position on the oversized sofa, she waved a dismissing hand. "Don't worry about dinner. I've been working at it all afternoon. First, I cook a little. Then I rest a little. Then I cook some more. The cake is in the oven along with the meat loaf—Roger's favorite."

He scooted her sideways with his hip and settled on the couch next to her. "Tell me exactly what the doctor said."

She lifted the hair off the back of her neck, then let it fall as she breathed a discouraged sigh. Fluttering down onto the padded couch arm, the mahogany hair was a pretty sight. The feel of her hip against his wasn't too bad, either.

"I'm having some early signs of premature labor, so the doctor said I should stop working, rest and drink plenty of fluids."

"Sounds more like the flu than premature labor."

Ariana wrinkled her nose at his attempted humor.

"According to my doctor, it's too early for the little wrestlers to make their grand entrance. They need more time to develop and grow."

Grant's stomach knotted. If anything happened to the twins, he would be to blame. "What else?"

"The longer I can hold on to them the fatter and healthier they will be. Even a week or two can make a big difference since having them now could mean respiratory problems or even long-term health issues." Her face took on that look Grant had come to recognize as determination. "I'll do everything in my power to assure these babies have a good start in life. So, here I am."

"And here you will stay. Have you given any thought of calling your mother?"

"I did call her, but I didn't *tell* her. I just needed to hear her voice." At his frown, she stuck her obstinate little nose in the air. "Now is not the time. Mama would be beside herself with fear."

Grant raked a hand down his face, catching his bottom lip between thumb and forefinger.

Since the moment Emily shared Ariana's home-bound status with him, an impulse had taken root and grown. Given his culpability and her refusal to bring her family into the picture, he saw no other choice.

"Somehow I knew you wouldn't tell her, stubborn woman. So." He paused for dramatic effect. "You're stuck with me."

Shocked almost to the point of silence—a rare event indeed—Ariana flopped back against the sofa arm. "I beg your pardon."

"Face the facts, Ariana. You need some help and I know you will not ask for it. So, I'm volunteering."

"Grant, I can't let you do that. You have a very busy job and a life of your own."

"A few weeks of dropping by in the evenings to help out will not be a problem. I don't mind. Truly." Couldn't she understand how much he needed to do this? Certain he'd caused the complication by dragging her off to Cape Cod, walking her all over the beach, and taking her out in a windswept boat, he owed her. If anything happened to her children because of him, he wasn't sure he could handle it.

"Why on earth would you make such an offer?"

He shrugged, though he'd asked himself the same question a dozen times in the last five minutes. Hiring someone to stay with her made more sense, but he chaffed at the notion of anyone else looking after her. She didn't need a hired stranger. She needed him.

"As your attorney, I—"

"This has nothing to do with your being my attorney." Ariana tried to lever up from the couch, but he pushed her down with one finger. "It doesn't make sense. It's unfair. I'll manage."

He crossed his arms and gave her his most imposing negotiator's stare. "How?"

"I don't know," she finally admitted, clearly miserable to be in such a position. "According to Dr. Knight, I'm stuck in this apartment except for trips to her office. And for my babies, I'll do that."

"Reasonable."

"But I have things to do, places to go."

"They'll have to wait."

"A person will starve unless she shops for groceries."

"I can shop."

"I have to fix my meals."

"I can cook."

"—And clean house."

"I can—" he grimaced "—hire someone."

Ariana laughed. "You're cute."

Grant allowed a grin. No one had called him cute since he was ten years old. "That's what you said to my niece."

"She's a different kind of cute." Ariana looked at him as though he'd rescued her from a sinking ship. "I don't know what to say except you're a very special man."

He lay a finger across her lips, then wished he hadn't. He'd tried to forget that night on the beach when he'd had the curious desire to kiss her. Now, at the touch of her soft, full lips, the urge returned in full force. But he hadn't come to kiss her; he'd come to take care of her.

"Don't say anything." His words came out in a hoarse whisper that didn't fit the occasion in the least.

"Your job is to rest and incubate. I will do everything else."

Except for the one thing he wanted to do most of all.

After three days Ariana was bored out of her mind with television and gestation. As much as she'd warned herself not to look forward to his arrival, and as many times as she'd told Grant he didn't *have* to come over, the man had gone out of his way to be available.

He telephoned at least twice daily, complete with office news and silly jokes that were entirely out of character, then arrived promptly each evening to putter around in her kitchen looking sexier with a white dish towel around his waist than he had without a shirt. And her palms still broke into a sweat at that memory. If the idea wasn't preposterous, Ariana would almost believe Grant cared for her.

"What did you do today?" Setting two cups of cocoa on the coffee table in front of her, he eyed the open laptop. "Not working, are you? I talked with personnel and they have you covered until after the first of the year."

"Dr. Knight said tying up loose ends at the office would be less stressful than not, but I'm only doing the things that can be done on-line." She hit Save and closed the lid. "One of my girlfriends has taken my place helping out at the senior citizens center and I've temporarily resigned my voluntary position at the halfway house. So here I lay, useless as chewed gum."

She and her couch had become much more intimately acquainted than she'd ever wanted to be. She stretched trying to relieve the nagging backache.

"Is your back hurting again?"

"What do you mean, again?"

Expression both sympathetic and amused, Grant untied and neatly folded his dish towel, then knelt beside the sofa. "Turn over on your side."

"Why?" But she shifted, facing the back of the couch.

"I'll give you a back rub."

Every nerve ending and all the latent sexual hormones that should have been sublimated by her outrageous state of pregnancy reacted. Ariana fought the response. It was only a back rub. A pair of hands kneading overtaxed muscle. A clinical, impersonal act.

That pair of hands pressed the small of her back. "Here?" his voice rumbled.

"Mmm. Hmm." She felt the effects in the strangest places. Really, this was ridiculous. She had to think of something else. She said the first thing that popped into her mind.

"Tell me about Tiffany." Not that Grant's ex was any of her business, but the woman had haunted Ariana from the moment she'd seen that gorgeous face.

The strong fingers hesitated. "How do you know about my ex-wife?"

"Vanessa showed me a photo of her." And I felt like a moose beside a gazelle.

He resumed the back rub, but his movements were laced with tension. "Tiffany's very beautiful. She lights up a room."

His declaration hurt, like a jab to the kidney. So he was still in love with her.

"Your mother says the two of you were perfect together."

Grant's fingers tightened. "Hardly, but we didn't realize how different we were until the damage was done.

I'm a homebody, who prefers a small circle of good friends rather than a hoard of casual acquaintances. Tiffany is the polar opposite, very social, always on the move."

"Nothing wrong with either of those styles."

"No, but after a while, she decided I was too dull to fit into her lifestyle. Stuffy, she called me."

"Dull?" Ariana heard the pain in his voice. So that explained his reaction to Vanessa's teasing. Ariana twisted around to face him. "What are you talking about? You aren't dull. Reserved at times, maybe, but more fun than any man I've ever known."

He cocked an eyebrow, voice wry. "Tiffany didn't agree with your assessment. And she found Cape Cod as boring as me."

"You're kidding?"

"Tiffany loved attention and was beautiful enough to get it anywhere there were people, so she wanted a crowd around her all the time. A peaceful sail on Nantucket Sound with only me wasn't enough. I wasn't enough."

Ariana heard the ache, the suffering his beautiful ex-wife had caused. How could she have found fault with such a fine man?

"So what happened? Did you just drift apart?"

His eyes slid away as he disappeared into a painful memory. "She found someone who wasn't so dull. I knew something was wrong between us but ignored the signs for a very long time. Too long."

Ariana lay a hand on his arm, sympathy thickening her voice. "Being cheated on hurts."

His eyes came back to hers. "You know that as well as I do."

"At least I found out the truth about Benjy before

we married. You had every reason to believe your wife would be faithful.''

''She blamed me for that, for her infidelity. And for her unwillingness to have children.''

''That makes no sense.''

''It did to her, and maybe she was right. Maybe I wasn't cut out to be a husband and father. I can be a bit of a loner at times. Maybe I didn't give her enough attention. Maybe a child *would* wither up and die of boredom in my care.''

''Oh, Grant.'' Every cell in Ariana's body cried for him. How could a woman be so callous—and so blind? ''Surely you didn't buy into that?''

He laughed, but the sound held no humor. ''The real kick in the teeth came after she took me to the cleaners in the divorce settlement. A year after the divorce she had a baby with another guy.'' He stared at the wall, voice tortured with the memory. ''She wouldn't have a child with me, but she did with him.''

Ariana swallowed a painful lump of compassion. ''So, that's why you're so turned off to marriage.''

''Exactly.''

''You must have loved her very much.''

He nodded slowly. ''Totally bedazzled. A beautiful woman can do funny things to a man's reason.''

Ariana's heart sank lower than an Alaskan sunset at Grant's admission. A man couldn't get much more in love than ''totally bedazzled.'' ''I'm sorry. You didn't deserve to be hurt that way.''

''What about you?'' He handed her the cooled cup of chocolate. ''Did you love Benjy?''

Turnabout was fair play. ''I thought I did. I wanted to. In the back of my mind I always had reservations, but I thought I could make our relationship work, especially after I got pregnant.'' She'd found out quickly that passion burns out when there's no depth to sustain it. ''But Benjy was furious. He was jealous of the twins from the get-go, hating the idea that I wouldn't be at his beck and call 24-7. He expected me to take care of him, not a couple of crying, smelly babies. And even though he promised marriage, our relationship went downhill from that moment.''

His cup clattered against saucer. ''He actually said those things?''

''Oh, yes. Those and many more. In fact, he asked me to—'' Having said more than she intended, she averted her gaze to sip the sweet, warm cocoa.

''Asked you to do what, angel?'' His voice went soft.

An unexpected tear burned behind her nose, whether from the endearment or the memory of Benjy's cruelty. She'd never admitted to anyone what her first and only lover had expected her to do with their babies.

''To—to—'' Swinging her gaze back to his, the ugly words tumbled out. ''To get rid of them.''

Grant's blue eyes turned glacial. A muscle in his jaw jerked, but the knuckle he stroked along her cheek was ever so gentle. ''And you couldn't do that, could you? No matter how inconvenient the timing, you love these little ones far too much.''

''Yes, I do.'' Grateful for his understanding, Ariana raised up, drawing him into a hug. He stiffened for a moment, then relaxed, pulling her upper body against his, stroking her back with his long hands.

The steady, dependable thump of his heart patted her cheek as she absorbed his strength and breathed in his masculine essence. Tears clogged her throat. Having someone to talk to and to lean on felt so good she wanted to stay in his arms forever.

But forever was not in the cards. After a moment, she reluctantly pulled back. "Thank you, Grant."

A quizzical smile tugged at the corners of his mouth. "For what?"

"For listening. For coming here. For putting up with my mood swings."

"Thank you for putting up with my cooking." He tapped her on the end of the nose. "Drink up your cocoa, I have to go. You need your rest."

She stifled a yawn. "Even with all this lying around, I am sleepy."

Eyes half closed, Ariana watched Grant's tall, lean body shrug into a black leather jacket. Like her, he'd been wounded in the line of love. Beneath the outward facade of togetherness, Mr. Perfect dealt with his own painful issues.

When she moved as if to see him out, he glared at her, a pleasant glare that made her insides grin even as she slid back into place on the couch, feet up, belly relaxed and back mercifully eased.

He took the shopping list from the bar and moved to the door. "Call if you need anything." He pointed a finger. "And behave yourself."

Regardless that he'd revealed his inner struggle, Mr. Perfect wanted her to know he was still very much in control.

Smiling her reply, she waited for to him leave, waited for the jiggle of the door as he double-checked the lock, then tiptoed to the door and strained to hear his footsteps down the hall.

She found herself leaning on Grant's strength in a way she'd never leaned on anyone. He was that kind of man, a novelty in her life. She'd always been the strong one, but now when she needed someone so badly, Grant had been there for her. She, the nurturer, needed Grant's nurturing.

She, who could pick the only loser out of a crowd of thousands, had stumbled onto a winner. Grant was without exception the finest man she'd ever known.

And that's when she understood why she let him come here night after night. And why she'd gone to Cape Cod. And why his beautiful ex-wife made her feel so fat and ugly.

She was in love with Grant Lawson. Not the kind of desperate emotion that grew out of pity or compassion, or the hot, aching physical hunger that burned out and left one empty, but real love. Steadfast and humbling and beautiful.

This was what love was supposed to have been; what it could be between a man and woman. Caring, trusting, sharing. Doing for one another out of joy, rather than pity or duty.

Banging her head against the door, she realized the terrible truth. She'd finally found her heart's desire after it was too late.

Chapter Eight

By the time Grant left his office the next day and headed for Ariana's apartment the early darkness of autumn had descended and a chill wind blew in from the harbor. The day had proven hectic, made worse by the phone call from his father inviting him to dinner. He knew what that was all about—more pressure to join the firm, but he'd begged off, citing previous plans. In the end, they'd agreed on a night next week which meant he needed to make a definitive decision between now and then. He'd also have to leave Ariana to her own devices for an evening, something he didn't want to do.

All day he'd thought of her, of their conversations the night before and the powerful pull of emotion between them. He'd told her things he'd never told anyone, and he had feeling she'd done the same.

Maybe the personal contact from the back massage had created a sense of intimacy. From that direction Ariana didn't even look pregnant and the rounded swell of bottom mere millimeters from his fingertips had been a temptation that made him sweat. But her body alone wasn't the cause of his disquiet. He enjoyed her company, liked her ideas, and loved her laughter.

What was it about her that compelled him, usually so detached from nonfamily members, to do and say things so out of character? And why did he get this sense of renewed energy knowing he was on the way to see her?

She was the first person outside his family to generate a warm emotional response in him in a very long time. He cared about her, but he hoped that was all. She deserved better than a man who had already proved less than adequate in male-female relationships.

He climbed the stairs to Ariana's apartment, tapped softly on the door, then using the key she'd given him, let himself inside. Having been here so often lately, the action felt like coming home, but he refused to follow that line of thinking.

As he stepped through the door, an orange throw pillow hit him in the chest. Ariana's laughter followed.

"I've always wanted to do that." Grinning at him from an easy chair, dark hair spilling around her shoulders, she took his breath away.

"Great weapon if you ever have a break-in." He returned fire, tossing the pillow much more gently so that it whapped softly against the side of her chair.

She made a face. "Sissy throw."

"You wait, woman, until there are no innocent children in the line of fire and I'll show you a real pillow fight."

"Promises, promises. I am *soooo* scared." She gave her eyes a playful roll that made him laugh.

"Do I detect the scent of seafood in this apartment?" He shot her a warning glare.

"Yes, but before you scold, I didn't do the cooking. One of my girlfriends brought over a pot of clam chowder and a loaf of brown bread this afternoon. Both are hot and ready to eat."

"Good. The weather's turned cold out there tonight." He shrugged out of his coat, draping it over the back of a chair. Then he went into the kitchen to dish up the chowder. "So how was your day?"

"Dreadful." Wearing a gray sweat suit and looking like a jogger hiding a basketball under her shirt, Ariana toddled in behind him. "Got so bored, a telemarketer hung up on me for keeping her on the phone too long."

"You're joking."

Her eyes sparkled with humor. "Yes, I am. Actually, today was my least boring day. Carrie came over with the chowder, Mrs. Porter popped by and several friends, including your sister telephoned."

The last surprised him. He set the steaming bowls on the table along with the sliced bread and two glasses of milk. He'd pestered Ariana about the calcium enough that she didn't even complain anymore. "What's Vanessa up to?"

"Checking on you, I think."

"On me?"

"In part. We had a great chat, but when she discovered I was homebound, she asked if you were spending a lot of time over here."

"Ah, I see." When she was seated at the table, he scooted the ottoman beneath her sock-encased feet. "She must have heard that I declined dinner with Dad tonight, and put two and two together. My sister is very perceptive."

"You had an offer for dinner with your father? Grant, why didn't you go?"

"I had a previous engagement with you so I took a rain check. Dad only wants to pressure me about the job anyway."

She took a bite of her chowder, made a little moan of appreciation, then said, "What are you going to do about that?"

"I haven't decided." Wanting to hear her thoughts on the matter, he regarded her over his spoon. "What do you think I should do?"

"Well, let's talk pros and cons. First, tell me the pros."

He'd made this list a dozen times. "Great money, instant respect and recognition, and most importantly, I'd be making my father very happy."

"Okay. Now the cons."

"I already make plenty of money, I'm fairly well respected in my field, I don't want to practice trial law and I have no interest in the social expectations that go with such a position, particularly the schmoozing." He shuddered at the thought. "Dad enjoys that aspect. I abhor it."

She pointed her spoon at him. "The real issue is not the job then, is it? The problem is your love for your father. You feel as if you'll let him down, as if you already have let him down by not being like him."

"Thank you, Sigmund, for that analysis." Even though he teased, he recognized the truth in her words. He'd always felt inadequate as an attorney, maybe even as a man, because his father was Royce Lawson.

"You are a fabulous attorney, gifted in corporate law and very comfortable there. You're you. You don't have to be him. The world needs both of you exactly the way you are. So shouldn't your father understand that his dream and yours are not the same?''

''I've been weighing this decision for a couple of weeks now, coming to pretty much the same conclusions. Thank you for articulating everything so well.'' He pushed his empty bowl aside. ''You need to have a talk with your family, too.''

''I'm going to. Very soon. As soon as the babies come and I have everything back under control.''

''Procrastinator. That phone call won't get any easier.''

''Take your own advice, counselor.''

''Two weeks of consideration is not the same as eight months. You'll feel much better once your family knows about your little miracles.'' Leaving her to think about that, he indicated her dish. ''Are you through with your chowder?''

At her nod, he took the empty bowls to the dishwasher and wiped off the table, then retrieved a book from his jacket. ''Brought you a present.''

He'd spotted the small volume at the convenience store last night and knew the timing was right.

''Another present? Grant, you're spoiling us.'' Though she chastised, her eyes twinkled in the delight. ''What are we ever going to do without you?''

Not wanting to go there, he plunked the book onto the table in front of her.

Ariana blinked down at the paperback of baby names. ''You are a thoughtful man. I've been mulling over names forever but nothing sounds right so far.''

''One thing for certain, you can't go on calling them Hansel and Gretel.''

''Or little wrestlers.'' She smiled in agreement.

''So I figured we might as well make the decision

now while we have this time on our hands. Do we know what we're having yet?'' The slip of the tongue escaped her, but not him. A Freudian slip, he admitted. Didn't he wish he were the expectant father of twins? Wasn't that, in part, why he was here? Yes, he felt responsible after taking her to the Cape, but if he faced the truth, wasn't he living vicariously through Ariana, sharing her pregnancy, her babies, because he'd never have the experience otherwise?

''The doctor is fairly certain we have both a boy and a girl in here,'' She patted the mound that grew higher each day. ''The ultrasound on Wednesday could be more definite.''

''Sugar and Spice, huh?'' After rummaging for a pencil and paper, he pulled a chair around beside her and opened the book. Ariana smelled good as if she'd showered before his arrival, an activity he would be better off not thinking about, considering that Ariana was the sexiest pregnant woman on the planet. ''Have you thought of using family names?''

She nodded, stirring the scent of shampoo and gardenias. He tried not to enjoy the fragrance, then wondered why he should deny himself such a simple, innocent pleasure, and breathed her in.

''What do you think about Amelia? That's Mama's middle name.''

''I like it, as long as it's for the girl.''

She whopped him on the arm. ''Of course, silly. Other than that, I'm stuck. Let's make a list of boys' names.''

Over the next hour they pored over the names, adding the ones they agreed upon to the list. Though he wasn't certain it was his place to make such decisions,

Grant loved every minute of the task. He would never have this opportunity again.

"Look," he said, laying his finger on the page. "This one means beautiful. That might work for Amelia's middle name."

"Ooh, I like the meaning. What's the name?"

"Tiferet."

She laughed and slapped his hand. "Don't write that down."

He grinned, enjoying the light in her eyes and the lift in his stomach each time she giggled. A few minutes later they settled on Amelia Rose for the girl, but they took a while longer to agree upon the boy's name.

"How about Christopher?" Grant had always liked the name, but he'd been hesitant to offer it as a possibility.

"Christopher. That's perfect! Amelia Rose and Christopher something." Deep in thought, she gnawed her lip studying the short list of names. Suddenly her gorgeous eyes glowed the color of the ocean on a summer's day. "I have the perfect middle name. That is, if you don't mind."

"Why would I mind?"

"Because I'd like to name him Christopher Grant."

"What?" Wild elation tempered by humility jolted him. He nearly fell out of his chair.

"I won't if you don't want me to." She spoke quickly as if afraid of offending him.

"Ariana, I'm touched that you'd even consider naming your son after me, but I have a confession to make first. Christopher is my middle name. I've always liked it and thought you might, too."

"Oh. Grant Christopher. Christopher Grant." She

looked crestfallen. "You'll want those names for your own son some day."

He lay a hand over hers and said gently, "That isn't going to happen, Ariana. Not ever." The reminder hurt. "Use the name if you want."

These babies had become important to him, and he liked the idea of one of them carrying a version of his name.

"I want." She smiled and his whole world brightened. Like a kid with a new toy, she tried the names out. "Christopher and Amelia. Amelia and Christopher. I love them." She spoke to her belly. "What do you think, kids?"

"I think they're darn lucky to have you for a mother."

"They may not agree when they get here and have to sleep in cardboard boxes."

"What are you talking about?"

She rolled her eyes as though he should know the answer. "In case you've forgotten, counselor, I've been in a bit of a budget crunch lately, waiting to buy baby furniture with my most recent paycheck. Trouble is, I'm now homebound and can't go shopping."

Grant felt like kicking himself. He should have realized she needed baby things, but the thought never occurred—more proof of how little he knew about parenting.

"Have you thought of ordering on-line?"

"Now there's an idea. I have some catalogs, too. I could order from those." She started up from the table. "Will you help me choose?"

"Get the catalogs and let's have a look. We're so good at names, finding baby furniture should be a snap."

A different idea began to form, but Grant decided to keep this one to himself. Ariana loved surprises, so he'd give her one—a big one.

The deliveries started shortly after noon. Ariana argued with the first man that he had the wrong address, but after seeing the bill of sale, signed by Grant Lawson, she gave up. Grant was the most unpredictable man she'd ever met. How any woman could call him stuffy was beyond her.

"Says here to tell you not to unpack a thing." The delivery man read from the invoice, ripped off the sheet and handed it to Ariana. "The fella that bought this wants to do it hisself."

Ten minutes later, Mrs. Porter, the landlady, followed the second delivery up the stairs and stuck her curly gray head in to inquire what all the commotion was about. Upon seeing two huge cartons marked Baby Crib and hearing that Grant had procured them, her wrinkled lips broke into a grin.

"I told you he was the best one." Then she disappeared, and Ariana suspected she and Grant were about to become the target of some affectionate, if sadly misguided, gossip. As much as she longed for something more between the two of them, Grant had made his intentions as clear as a new window.

When the doorbell stopped ringing long enough, Ariana thought to call Grant and find out what on earth he was up to.

As she touched the phone, it rang.

"Hello."

"Ariana?"

"Grant, what do you think you are doing?" She heard voices in the background.

"Doing? I don't know what you mean." Laughter danced around the edge of his voice.

"Don't play innocent with me. You shouldn't be buying all these baby things. That's my job."

He knew her financial situation and had no business making purchases without her consent. She'd never be able to make the payments.

"But you can't shop."

She heard the voices again and this time Grant spoke to someone other than her. She couldn't quite make out the sounds, but they were not Wintersoft noises.

"Grant, where are you?"

"Some store called Perfect Baby. You should see this place. Everything you ever dreamed of for an infant."

Sliding down onto the sofa, she stared at the receiver in disbelief. "You didn't go to work today?"

"Work? No. I told them I had to go Christmas shopping."

Grant Lawson took a day off? He never missed work. "It isn't Christmas."

He chuckled and the sound flowed down her spine like warm oil. "It will be one of these days."

"Have you lost your mind?"

"I must admit a man could go crazy in a store like this. I am definitely the misfit." He seemed to be loving every minute of the experience. "I'm surrounded by round-bodied ladies, all of whom are more than willing to explain which booties stay on best and what thermometer is easiest to use. Did you know there are at least a half dozen types of bottle nipples?" He sounded awed. "Which brings me to a question they all keep asking. Breast or bottle?"

"Grant!" Heat rushed over her.

He must have heard the panic in her voice. "Okay, then. I'll get bottles for backup until you decide."

"No, don't do that. You have to stop buying things. I can't afford them."

"I can." In an aside, she heard him say, "Oh, yeah, I'll take two of those, too."

"Grant, don't buy another thing!"

"I'll be home in a couple of hours. Go put your feet up."

"Did you hear me, Grant Christopher Lawson? Not another thing."

All she heard was laughter, then the line went dead.

She grabbed her address book, found his cell phone number and punched in the digits. Three tries later she left the same message on his voice mail. "Don't buy anything else."

She'd no more than hung up when her phone rang. "Hello."

"Really, Ariana," he teased with mock horror. "You must stop calling me at this number. People are beginning to talk."

"Grant. Do not buy another thing. I mean it."

More laughter. And dead air.

Exhilarated, overwhelmed, pulses pounding, Ariana didn't know what to do. That crazy, wonderful man. What was he thinking? And why was he going to such trouble for her and her babies? Didn't he understand that all this attention would only make her more miserable when it was over?

Hand against her chest to keep her heart from jumping out, she followed Grant's advice and lay down on the couch. Too much excitement was not good for the twins, and she was excited to say the least.

When Grant arrived, far earlier than usual, carrying

yet more boxes, bags, and cartons, Ariana rested dutifully on her left side, list in hand, trying to keep track of everything he'd purchased. The living-dining area looked like a UPS weigh station.

"I told you not to buy all this stuff." Her scowl didn't appear to affect him in the least.

Letting his packages tumble wherever an empty spot could be found, Grant picked his way around the cartons and grinned down at her. "Don't be mad. We had to prepare for the munchkins. They'll be here soon and I do believe you said something about them sleeping in cardboard boxes." Blue eyes twinkling, he spread his hands. "Now, you have plenty of boxes to choose from."

"I'm going to send most of this back. I can't afford so much."

Sliding down onto the couch beside her, some of the pleasure left his expression. "Ariana, you aren't sending anything back. These are gifts. I wanted to do this."

"But it isn't right."

"Please don't spoil my fun."

Ariana opened her mouth for further protest, but as she looked into Grant's face, she couldn't say another negative thing. Animated, excited, he was having the time of his life.

"You really did have fun doing this, didn't you?"

He took her itemized list and lay it on the coffee table, boyish grin still very much in place. Pride in the accomplishment radiated from him like a light.

"Like a kid in a candy store." He rubbed his palms together. "And now for the rest of the fun. Where do you want the nursery set up?"

"We don't have much choice." Her apartment was

small, including only one bedroom. "Somehow we'll have to rearrange the bedroom."

"I took that into consideration during my shopping spree."

She grinned, trying to associate shopping with Grant. The image wouldn't fit. "Do you know how funny that sounds?"

Returning her smile, he said, "I've never gone on a shopping spree in my life. Now I know why women say it's exhausting." Offering a hand, he pulled her to her feet. "You rest on the bed—*after* I move it, of course." He dodged when she took a playful swing at him. "You can supervise from there while I set things up."

She waddled into the bedroom, waited while he shoved the bed against the far wall, then lay down and watched him lug baby furniture into the room. The silly man had spent a small fortune. "If you ever manage to win support from Benjy you are to keep the money until all this is paid for."

Using a knife from the kitchen he ripped open the side of a box, then stared at her over the top. "Not another word about this, woman!"

As though terrified, she gave a mock shudder. "Okay, okay. But at least let me do something useful."

Grant disappeared into the living room and returned with a stack of packages. Perching on the edge of the bed, he pushed the boxes toward her. "The ladies at Perfect Baby helped me choose, but I tried to keep in mind the things you liked from the catalog. See what you think."

Ariana's heart did a little pitty-pat. Ever since the beginning of her pregnancy, she'd been buying a few baby items now and then when she could, but in one day Grant had erased all her concerns about providing for the twins arrival.

"I bought a lot of pink and blue, but that might become too *boring*." Eyes widening in self-ridicule, he made quotation marks in the air. "So, I also chose every other color available." He reached into one bag and took out two bright red onesies complete with hats and booties. "This color is especially for you."

Since discovering her propensity for bright colors, he'd gone out of his way to surround her with them. Flowers, balloons, and now this.

"I love that! Did they have any lime-green?"

For the hundredth time Ariana thought about Grant's ex-wife's assertion that he was too stodgy to be a husband and father. Foolish woman. She'd never known him at all.

With a flourish, Grant whipped out a set of footed pajamas. "These are so lime they are guaranteed to glow in the dark."

Giggling, Ariana took the soft, cotton nighties and pressed them against her cheek. "I won't even need a night-light."

"Got one of those, too." He glanced around at all the cartons, then tossed his hands up in surrender. "Somewhere."

Ariana peeked into one bag after another, so full of joy she could hardly breathe. "If you'll hand me the drawers from the chest, I can put these clothes away as I unpack them."

"Are you sure it won't be too much for you?"

"I have learned to do most everything while lying down."

Grant lifted one eyebrow. "A woman of many talents."

My, he was in a delightful mood tonight. Shopping agreed with him.

"I'll get these cribs set up," he said, then held up a finger as if to stop himself. "But first the music."

At Ariana's questioning look, he explained, "Listening to Mozart is supposed to increase a baby's intelligence. Right? So I bought these CDs. Gotta have smart babies!"

Ariana could only stare. Did the man think of everything?

He pushed play on the CD player and the silvery strains of Mozart filled the room. Then he went to work, turning one section of her bedroom into an infant's haven.

In the meantime, Ariana opened boxes and bags, amazed at the layette he'd purchased. Booties, bibs, bottles. Diapers, blankets, sleepers, many exactly like the ones she'd pointed out in the catalogs, though he'd bought far more than she'd chosen. She exclaimed over each new item as she sorted, folded, and placed it into the drawer.

When at last Grant sat back on his haunches, satisfaction seeped from every handsome pore. The convertible sleigh cribs were erected and adorned with adorable teddy bear bedding in primary colors. Over each one a colorful mobile circled, Brahms' lullaby competing with the Mozart. And he'd arranged everything, from the cribs to the combination chest/changing table to the cozy rocking chair so that she could move around the bedroom.

"Everything looks incredible." Ariana clasped her hands over her chest, partly out of joy, partly to still the excited dancing of her heart.

"It does, doesn't it?" Gathering his tools, he stepped

back to proudly survey his work, Mozart swelling around them with the same rich intensity as the swelling of Ariana's love. Grant looked for all the world like a proud papa.

Hair mussed, shirt sleeves rolled up, this strong, witty, spontaneous, and utterly gorgeous man deserved the happiness Tiffany had denied him. He had a storehouse of love, dying to be released. Regardless of his argument to the contrary Grant deserved a loving woman and children upon whom to shower all that repressed emotion.

If he had loved her the way he loved Tiffany, she would have built her world around him.

Oh, Grant, she thought, *why couldn't I have met you first, before it was too late for both of us?*

Chapter Nine

Ariana seldom complained, but tonight when Grant had arrived, she was already in bed, wearing her pajamas. Prepartum blues, she'd called her moodiness, trying to laugh off the symptoms, but Grant saw behind the changeable eyes to a deep weariness.

They'd had such a good time last night arranging the baby furniture and sorting through the tiny clothing. Now, he wondered if his overzealous attempt to provide for the twins had jeopardized them in some way.

If not for her appointment with the obstetrician tomorrow, he'd have loaded her in the Lexus and driven to the E.R.

Instead he rubbed her back, read to her from Dr. Spock, told her every knock-knock joke he could remember, and finally, retired to the kitchen to open a can of tomato soup—the only food she'd agree to eat. He was pouring the steaming soup into oversize mugs when the telephone rang. Knowing she had an extension in the bedroom, he let her answer and went back to work.

Hoping to cheer her, he added bright red napkins and a candle to the meager dinner tray. As he approached the bedroom, he could hear her talking. Quietly he pushed the door open.

Looking up, she glanced him in the doorway and waved him inside.

"Everything is great here, Mama," she said into the phone. "No, nothing's wrong. I'm a little tired tonight. That's all."

Her mother. The perfect opportunity to take a load of worry off her shoulders. He raised his eyebrows, nodded at her bulging stomach, and mouthed, "Did you tell her?"

Frantically, eyes widening, she shook her head. "No. Benjy and I didn't work things out, but I'm okay. He wasn't the right man for me."

Grant's gut knotted. Benjy not only wasn't right for her, but he was also pond scum. Grant knew if he'd been fortunate enough to love this beautiful woman and to be the father of her twins, no power on earth could have kept him from her side.

He eased closer to the bed and whispered. "Tell her."

Ariana stubbornly averted her face. "Yes, I know I'm the strong one. That's why you needn't concern yourself. Life is perfect here in Boston. Mmm-hmm. Christmas? Oh, I hope so, Mama. Okay. Give everyone my love. I love you, too. Bye."

She hung up the phone and burst into tears.

Grant nearly dropped the soup tray. Shoving the meal onto the lamp table, he sat down on the bed and pulled her into his arms. "Hey, don't do that." Her tears ripped him apart. "Hush now."

She took a few gulping breaths and buried her face in his shirt.

"Why can't I tell her?" The sobbing words were warm and muffled against his chest. "I wanted to. I intended to, but the words wouldn't come out."

He stroked her hair, comforting her as he would his niece though the emotion hammering at his insides was not even close to the same. "You're scared. That's all. You'll find a way."

"No, I won't. I'm a liar. A big, fat, ugly liar."

He battled the smile that threatened. Sounding every bit as childish as his niece, Ariana was under siege from her hormones. "Ariana, you are not big and you are not fat. And the only time you lie is to keep from hurting others." He'd been relieved to figure that out about her. "But sooner or later, you'll realize that you hurt them more by lying than by telling them the truth. You certainly hurt yourself in the process."

She pulled back a little, but Grant didn't let her go. She needed his arms around her, whether she knew it or not. And he needed them there.

"So why can't I stop? Why can't I say, 'Mama, I was pregnant when Benjy left me'?"

He'd wrestled with her dilemma for a while, listening to her troubled explanations and excuses. Now, he'd take his turn playing junior psychologist. Drying her tears with his thumbs, he spoke gently. "Could the trouble be that you have this picture in your mind of the perfect daughter who never gives her parents a moment of concern and now you're afraid of what they'll think?"

"Is that what I'm doing? Am I so shallow that I'm

protecting some made-up image of myself?'' Fresh
tears welled in her eyes. ''All I ever wanted was for
my family to be proud of me.''

''They are proud of you, angel.'' He brushed loose
strands of hair away from her teary face. ''Stop selling
yourself short. You're an extraordinary woman. Half of
Boston could testify to that.''

Why couldn't she understand how special she was?
Caring for senior citizens, befriending her neighbors,
volunteering her time. Not to mention the excellent
work she did at Wintersoft and the number of people
who called her friend.

''But I've made so many mistakes. Benjy—''

He cut her off, surprised at his harsh reaction. ''Forget Benjy.''

If he never heard the man's name again, it would be
too soon. He wanted the ex to disappear and never
bother Ariana or these babies. Though Grant had no
right to think such thoughts, he wanted to take care of
her, to protect her, to give her everything she needed.

Benjy be hanged. His rejection had done a number
on Ariana's self-esteem.

Someone needed to show her how incredible—and
desirable—she was.

Before the knowledge of his intention reached his
brain, Grant took Ariana's face in his hands. Her eyes
went wide, softening perceptibly, as he pulled her to
him. He'd considered doing this more than once, and
the reasons didn't matter. He was a man. She was a
woman. And maybe, just maybe if he kissed her once,
this great yearning inside him would go away.

Slanting his mouth over hers, he tasted the sweetness
he'd wondered about for weeks. With a frightening
surety, he knew once would not be enough.

After a sharp intake of breath, Ariana gave a little sigh and returned the kiss.

The earth shifted beneath him. The universe tilted. His knees trembled with a startling desire, not only for sex, though heaven knew he wanted her in that way, too, but a desire for all the missing elements in his life that she fulfilled. Impossible, intolerable desire.

When the kiss ended, he drew back with a ragged sigh, longing for more, but knowing better. Ariana looked bemused…and troubled. He cursed his inconsiderate male hormones. The last thing he intended to do was to hurt this fragile angel.

"I'm sorry, Ariana. I shouldn't have done that."

"It was only a kiss." But she looked ready to cry again.

No, it wasn't only a kiss. But he couldn't think exactly what it was. "I don't want you to get the wrong idea. I never intended—"

Frustrated, he shoved a hand through his hair. How did he make her understand that while he was good at a lot things, he was less than adequate in personal relationships? He wasn't good at reading a woman's moods or understanding her deepest needs. Hadn't Tiffany told him that a hundred times? That he was a stiff, unfeeling cad who couldn't think past his law books? And hadn't he proven the accusation by kissing Ariana when she was already upset?

"Grant." She pressed her fingertips to his mouth. They trembled against his lips, and he barely resisted the urge to kiss her again. "It's okay. I understand."

Well, he certainly didn't.

Lips tingling with the memory of Grant's kiss, blood still singing even while her heart ached, Ariana wished she could vanish into thin air. The kiss that had meant everything to her meant nothing to him.

And why should it? He was trying to comfort her in a time of stress. Mr. Perfect, playing nice. That was all.

Suddenly exhaustion invaded every cell. She didn't want to think or talk. And if Grant didn't go away, she'd make a total fool of herself and likely end their friendship by confessing her love.

Tearing her hand from the pleasant stubble of his cheek, she lay back, scooting under the blankets. "If you don't mind I'll skip the soup and go to sleep now."

Expression concerned, Grant stood, uncertain. "Are you okay?"

She managed a weak smile. "Fine. Tired." Then using the handy excuse, she placed a palm on her abdomen and said, "Resting up for the big moment."

"All right, then." Blue eyes swept over her, searching, puzzled at her change of mood. "I'll clean up in the kitchen and let myself out."

With a tenderness that brought a lump to her throat, he tucked the cover beneath her chin, his manly scent hovering over her as warm as the flannel blanket.

His breath, sweet scented and warm from the cocoa she hadn't wanted, brushed her cheek. He hovered there for a moment, and she had the anticipatory sense that he might kiss her again. But the moment passed. He moved away, snapping off the light. Disappointment nearly as strong as grief shimmied through her.

He'd never intended to kiss her in the first place. Hadn't he told her that, and yet she lay here like a needy child longing for him to feel something that he clearly didn't. Why would Mr. Perfect, a man with everything going for him fall in love with a dismal failure such as she?

Wrapping her arms around her little family, Ariana turned on her side, praying for sleep that wouldn't come and an answer to her uncertain future.

Grant hung up the telephone and relaxed back against his executive chair, relief rushing through him with all the vigor of a spring wind. Though the last ten minutes hadn't been easy, he was glad to have the conversation with his father behind him. Watching Ariana's anxiety level increase with every passing opportunity to talk to her family had solidified his conviction that problems must be faced head-on. Procrastination only made things worse.

His father had taken the news well, considering how badly he wanted Grant to join the firm. But when Grant had protested that he wouldn't make a good trial lawyer, Dad had said the words that set him free. "I asked you, son, because I only wanted the best."

From that moment forward Grant knew he'd made the right decision. He *was* a good lawyer, good enough to work for Dad's firm if he chose. But remaining true to himself was better for everyone, including his father.

Going to the window, he gazed out at Boston Harbor. A couple of die-hard sailors struggled against a north wind that promised colder weather. The water was choppy, the sky gray and overcast.

His mind went to Ariana, confined to her apartment now for nearly two weeks. Dreary weather didn't bother her, but after last night he worried about her emotional condition. Like an idiot, he'd kissed her, then lay awake half the night, wondering what had come over him.

Her trust in him, even after her worthless ex wronged her, moved him like nothing else. She made him feel like a man in a way he hadn't in years. As a businessman, he was confident and competent, cool as ice and ultraprofessional. There was no case he couldn't win. No area of expertise he couldn't attain. But since Tiffany's cruel form of emasculation, his personal life, other than with his immediate family, had become a vacuum. Somehow, sweet Ariana had changed that. Drawing him in like a warm fire on a frosty night, she filled him. Filled his mind and his time.

Good intentions warred with common sense. Common sense said get away from her as fast as possible before the attachment grew any more dangerous, but he'd made a promise to be with her until the twins arrived, and he never backed away from a commitment.

His intercom buzzed, momentarily sidetracking his thoughts of Ariana. Before he could respond, his office door burst open and a man stormed in, anger radiating off him like sunlight off aluminum.

"Are you Lawson?"

Usually fair-minded, Grant experienced an instant dislike for this guy. Far too old for the look, he dressed like an Ivy League frat boy. Brown hair flopped over his forehead in what Grant assumed to be his boyishly handsome pose. And his mouth turned down in a put-upon, pity-me frown.

"I'm Grant Lawson. What can I do for you?" Grant came around the desk, but he didn't offer his handshake. He checked his Rolex, letting his unexpected visitor know that time was of the essence. Ariana had a doctor's appointment, and if he was late, the stubborn woman would take the bus.

"You can get off my back. That's what you can do."

Arching one eyebrow, Grant nailed him with his most imposing stare. "And you are?"

"Benjamin Walburn. My boss is giving me fits because of you. Threatening to hold my check or fire me unless you stop hounding him."

Dislike turned to something far stronger. So this was the lowlife who'd hurt Ariana and abandoned his own offspring.

With icy professionalism, Grant replied, "Lest you forget, Mr. Walburn, you have an obligation to care for your unborn children. That's all Ms. Fitzpatrick is asking."

"My children?" He made a scoffing noise that set Grant's teeth on edge. "Let me tell you something about that, mister. Ariana's got no business laying this rap on me. I'm just the fall guy."

The muscle in Grant's jaw tightened. "What exactly are you implying about my client?"

Benjy sneered. "I'm not implying anything. I'm saying it right out. Those twins of hers could have belonged to a half dozen different guys. Ariana was anybody's anytime." He tossed the hair off his forehead. "Get the picture? Or do I need to spell it out for you?"

All the air whooshed out of Grant as though he'd been sucker-punched. Ariana with other men. The pent-up energy drained away, leaving him empty, bereft. Hadn't he worried about this very thing? In spite of her sweetness, Ariana was as faithless and dishonest as Tiffany.

As quickly as the thought came, Grant knew it was a lie. He'd spent every day for weeks with her and knew she was as pure a heart as he'd ever known. She would never do that to a man. Never. Her white lies had always been to spare someone, not to hurt them. Ariana was incapable of such cruel, hurtful deceit.

Straightening, Grant stared down his nose at Benjy Walburn. "I think it's time for you to leave, Mr. Walburn."

The scum would do or say anything to benefit his own selfish agenda, including maligning the pure and lovely woman he was supposed to have cared for—the mother of his children.

"What's the matter, Lawson? Mad because she's too fat and pregnant to be of any use to you?"

A primal urge to squash the life out of this cockroach roared inside Grant's head. He considered himself an extremely civilized man. He hadn't punched anyone since he was twelve years old. Hands fisted at his sides, he slowly began counting to ten. He got all the way to three. Then he shocked them both by wiping the smirk off Benjy's petulant mouth.

Benjy stumbled backward into the office wall. The picture of Grant's favorite sailboat rattled loose and fell to the floor. Grant felt more contrition over the broken frame than he did the man's bleeding mouth. With complete contempt, Grant jerked a handful of Kleenex from his desk and shoved them at Benjy. "Don't bleed on the furniture on your way out, Mr. Walburn."

"You owe me, big shot. I'm going to sue."

Grant advanced on him again. "Get…out!"

Scrambling sideways, eyes wide and frightened enough to give Grant a certain perverse pleasure, Benjy found the door, wrenched it open and disappeared down the corridor.

Blood racing, Grant stood for a moment staring after him. Then, taking a deep breath, he straightened his tie, checked his throbbing knuckles for injury and set his desk in order for the weekend.

Taking his briefcase, he strode to the elevator. Still flushed and hot and sizzling from his encounter with Benjy, Grant hoped he didn't meet anyone on the way out. The drive to Ariana's would give him time to calm down.

Fortunately the only person he saw in the corridor was Emily Winters and she was too far away for conversation. The boss's daughter lifted a hand in greeting before proceeding into her father's office.

Emily noticed Grant Lawson's uncharacteristically disheveled appearance and the fact that he appeared to be leaving early, but considered neither to be any of her business. Grant was the consummate professional, did an outstanding job for Wintersoft, Inc., and if he chose to leave work early on a rare occasion, so be it. He put in plenty of extra hours when needed.

With a soft rap, she opened the door to her father's office and stepped inside to find him engaged in conversation with Jack Devon. The handsome senior vice president of Business Development and Strategy rose briefly from his chair.

"Emily."

"Hello, Jack." Emily nodded coolly, then turned to her father. Still movie star handsome at sixty-two, Lloyd's blue eyes and silver hair distinguished him in any crowd. "Am I interrupting something?"

"Not at all, Em. I was just inviting Jack to the dinner party." Lloyd turned an approving look on the other man, a look that caused a surprising pinch of jealousy in Emily. Lately, every time she'd seen Jack and her father together, Jack had been treated as the favored son. Though she knew her father loved her deeply, she couldn't shake the idea that he'd have preferred a son instead of a daughter.

"You're still planning to come, too, aren't you, Emily?" her father asked.

"Of course. I wouldn't miss it."

"Good, good. I'm eager to meet this friend of yours, Stephen. Isn't that his name?"

Instant anxiety, mingled with the ever-present guilt, zipped through Emily. Stephen, as dear as he was, could never pull off the dinner party without revealing his true nature. Father would know in a New York minute that Stephen would never be a candidate for her hand in marriage.

Her gaze flickered to Jack's. What she saw there increased her anxiety. Speculation, humor even, sparkled in his gray eyes. No doubt he *knew* the truth. He'd met Stephen the night of the charity ball.

"Um, no. Actually, Father, Stephen and I have agreed to see other people. He won't be coming." Despising the need for subterfuge she, nevertheless, could not allow Father to interfere in her relationships again.

"I'm bringing someone else. Marco Valenti." Marco had been after her to go out with him for months. Now she'd have to accept.

Her father's disappointment turned to interest.

Jack, on the other hand, jerked upright in his chair, distaste written on every feature. "Marco Valenti!"

"Excuse me?" Emily blinked in surprise at Jack's negative reaction to her choice of dates. "Is there a problem?"

Looking discomfited by his outburst, Jack shrugged and lounged back into the chair. "No. No problem at all. Other than Valenti doesn't seem to be your type."

"Now, Jack," her father interjected. "Emily is a fine judge of character." He turned his smile on her. "I'll look forward to meeting this Valenti fellow. He must be someone special."

Guilt shafted through her. She hated lying to her father and flaunting pretend boyfriends, but she hated the alternative more. As long as one Wintersoft bachelor executive remained, she was compelled to continue the charade. Otherwise, Father would embarrass them both by playing matchmaker, and ruin his own reputation as a sensible businessman. He'd worked too hard for that to happen, and Emily did not plan to be the cause of such a tragedy.

Chapter Ten

Surrounded by more pregnant women than he'd ever seen in his life, Grant leafed through a parenting magazine, the only male in the waiting area. Next to him in a green vinyl chair Ariana waited to be called for her ultrasound. She was herself today, much to his relief, showing no aftereffects from last night's crying jag or from the kiss that should never have occurred.

She'd been on an emotional roller coaster lately: the pregnancy, her family and the child support case. Hiding his bruised and reddened knuckles against his thigh, Grant decided not to tell Ariana about Benjy's ugly accusations. The stress might further jeopardize the babies.

Head bent over a magazine, her shining mahogany hair swung forward to caress her lovely profile. Deep in concentration, she gnawed a fingernail. Grant reached out, brushed her hair back, holding the silken locks against her scalp. She angled a questioning smile in his direction.

"What are you reading?"

She tilted the article toward him, and he caught the subtle scent of flowers. "Did you know that women in Massachusetts are twenty-five percent more likely to give birth to twins than women in other states?"

"Can't say that I did." Her intensity amused him. She was so focused on these babies, so set on knowing everything possible about them. Her apartment overflowed with child care books. He should know; he'd read most of them with her.

"And," she frowned. "Eighty percent of the time, one twin or another—usually the second one—is turned funny and has trouble being delivered."

He didn't much like the sound of that. "We fully expect to be in the twenty percent minority, don't we?"

"Yeah. We sure do." Looking down, she bracketed her belly with both hands. "Hear that, kids? No funny stuff."

"What did your doctor say? Does she foresee any complications of that nature?"

She shook her head, hair dancing around her shoulders. "Everything is right on target. Apparently these boring two weeks of doing nothing has helped the babies grow and thrive. Even if they came early they should do fine."

"But she does expect you to carry them full term, doesn't she?"

"So far so good. No further signs of premature labor." She grinned at him. "You, counselor, can take credit for that. Two weeks of nagging me to put my feet up and drink milk, shopping for baby furniture and telling bad jokes has paid off."

"Hey. Who says my jokes are bad?" He pretended offense for the express purpose of watching her smile.

They were grinning like two kids when the technician appeared, dressed in green scrubs and carrying a clipboard. "We're ready for you, Ms. Fitzpatrick."

Grant stood, offered her a hand out of the chair.

"Ah-ha," she teased, eyes sparkling green above her burgundy blouse. "So you do think I'm fat."

"Overloaded. Never fat." He pulled her to her feet.

"Spoken like a wise attorney." She pecked him on the shoulder with a finger, then started forward following the tech. As he moved to sit down again, she paused and turned. "Would you like to come with me? See your namesake?"

Jolted by the idea, Grant hesitated. But the hunger to see the twins, to share one more significant moment with Ariana proved too tempting. Refusing to consider the wisdom of his actions, he nodded and clasped her outstretched hand.

Inside the narrow room, Ariana slipped off her shoes and climbed onto the table. The technician, like a green clad magician, waved a wand over her bared belly.

Out of his element, Grant stood awkwardly beside her and concentrated on the amazing technology that would allow him to see the two little people inside Ariana's smooth, tanned body.

His stomach took a nosedive. Was he ready for this?

Before he could decide, the technician completed his adjustments and clicked on the monitor.

A rapid *flub-flub-flub* filled the room. Then another distinctive heartbeat joined the first, almost like clocks ticking though the sound was deeper, richer.

He'd never heard a fetal heartbeat and the sound filled him with wonder. His own heart thundered in comparison.

And then, as if by magic, two squirming images appeared on the screen, each tiny body curled in toward the other.

"Look. There they are," Ariana whispered as if afraid of waking the sleeping beauties.

"Why is one upside down?" He asked, tone equally hushed.

The tech, using a pointer, touched a spot on the screen. "That's a good thing. She's gearing up for the home stretch."

"She?" A smile bloomed in his chest. "So that's Amelia."

Ariana swiveled her head toward him. She looked beyond beautiful with her richly colored hair fanned out against the blinding white sheets. "And the little right-side-up floater must be Christopher."

"Christopher Grant." *Hey, buddy, little namesake.*

He couldn't tear his gaze away from the monitor. From the two tiny people, unblemished by life, pure and perfect, with the future spread out before them.

So this is how an expectant father felt—exultant anticipation mingled with stark terror. Would the delivery go well? Would the twins be healthy? Would the world be a decent place for them to grow up?

A well of something powerful and overwhelming rose, swelling to a crescendo that set off all kinds of alarms in his head. The need for self-preservation warred with the undeniable need to possess that which was not his to claim.

At some point he grappled for Ariana's hand atop the smooth white sheet. Here he stood, throat too full to speak, weak in the knees because of two tiny babies and one incredible woman.

The word love filtered through his mind, but he rejected it. Ariana had needed him, and for some purely psychological reason, he'd needed to be needed. Once that time passed, Ariana would walk away, returning to her independent lifestyle and taking her children with her. Inadequacy suffused him. As much as this moment moved him, he had no place in their future. They deserved better.

The sonographer's voice broke into his somber thoughts. "Hopefully, little Christopher will learn his directions soon and follow his sister's lead."

Leaving one disturbing thought for another, Grant remembered the complication of a baby turning the wrong direction. "Is that likely?"

"Not likely, but possible. Babies can turn anytime, sometimes even during delivery."

Ariana's fingers tensed in his. "What if he doesn't turn? What will happen?"

The man lifted a green-clad shoulder. "C-Section."

Eyes growing huge and luminous in the dim room, Ariana voice quavered. "That scares me."

Grant didn't want anything to frightened her. Ever. He leaned toward her, giving her a steadying smile.

"Hey, that's my namesake in there. Don't worry. He'll do the right thing when the time comes."

Ariana turned her attention to him, studying his strong, dependable, honest face. How she loved this man. Grant Lawson, Mr. Perfect, who would always do the right thing.

"If Christopher is anything at all like you, I will rejoice."

Grant leaned forward, smoothed back her hair and placed a soft kiss on her forehead. "That's a sweet thing to say."

His breath warmed her skin. His expensive sandalwood scent wrapped around her like a flannel blanket. But it was the touch of his lips to her skin that set Ariana's soul afire.

Every cell in her body reacted. Already hypersensitive from viewing the little ones, Grant's innocent kiss rocked her. After all her mistakes, all the times she'd tried to fix the lives of troubled boyfriends, here was a man who didn't need anything from her. He gave and gave, asking nothing in return. In truth, she had nothing to give him—nothing but her heart.

Nearly bursting with love for the little miracles on the screen and for the man who'd become more of a father to them than Benjy would ever be, she couldn't keep quiet any longer.

"I mean it, Grant. You're the best thing that ever happened to us." Eyes never leaving his face, she hitched her chin toward the monitor. "To them, and to me."

"I haven't done anything all that special." He tapped her nose, then let his finger slide down over her lips and chin. "You, on the other hand, have produced these two."

He raised his eyes to the monitor, and Ariana followed suit, deeply moved by his fascination for the twins.

"If I could live my life over," she whispered. "If I could do things differently…"

"Shh." He lay a finger on her lips and shook his head. "No regrets. Changing the past would change who you are today, and that would take away the twins. You don't want that, and neither do I."

She clasped his hand to her chest and held on, compelled to express the sentiment welling inside like a tidal wave. "You're right. I only wish…"

"I know, angel." Leaning over her, his voice went soft and deep. "I know."

Angel, he'd called her, and the endearment melted her, wrapping her in a cocoon of loving security.

"Do you?" She locked her gaze with his, and the world around them disappeared. How did she express what was inside her? How did she tell him of the enormous joy he'd brought into her life?

Mesmerized by the magical moment and a pair of blue eyes that saw into her soul, Ariana blurted the secret she'd tried so hard to keep. "Then you must know that I've wished a thousand times you were the father of these babies. I love you, Grant."

Grant's bemused, enraptured expression faded, replaced by wariness. Other than to blink bewildered eyes, he didn't move, but Ariana felt him drawing away. Her insides trembled at his shocked reaction. Hadn't he even suspected? Had she done the wrong thing? Ruined the sweet camaraderie between them?

"Ariana..." He struggled for words, an endearing furrow between his eyes. Honorable Grant, with his innate sense of correctness, didn't want to hurt her. With a sinking sensation, Ariana battled the urge to rush to his aid, to tell the easy lie and take back the words. But this time she couldn't, *wouldn't* deny the truth.

Grant cleared his throat, shifting his focus from the screen to the curious technician, then back to her. Confusion clouded his blue eyes. "I think that's your hormones talking."

And Ariana knew, with a painful certainty, that he didn't return her feelings. And why should he? He probably thought she was looking for a sugar daddy, someone to pick up the pieces of her life and provide a husband and father. Hadn't he been doing that for weeks now? Filling the roll, playing the part out of kindness. He hadn't meant anything by his actions. He'd only been Grant, doing the right thing.

The drive home was quiet, broodingly so, neither of them inclined to finish the troublesome conversation. Lost in thought, Ariana didn't see the buildings, or cars, or stoplights. She kept hearing her foolish tongue blurting words that Grant hadn't wanted to hear.

Grant pulled the car to a stop along the maple-lined curb in front of her apartment building and turned toward her. He draped a wrist over the steering wheel, Rolex gleaming in the sunlight. If she lived to be a hundred, the sight of a Rolex watch would always remind her of Grant.

"Are you okay?"

So this was his idea of continuing the conversation.

She swallowed the lump in her throat and did something totally uncharacteristic. She took the bull by the horns. "Grant, I handed you my heart on a silver platter and you handed it back. No, I'm not okay, but I will be."

The cool shuttered Grant, the one she hadn't seen in a long time, gazed at her. "Don't think I don't care about you, Ariana. I do."

And that admission hurt more than outright rejection. He cared for her, cooked for her, shopped for her, but he could not love her.

She, the worst judge of men on the planet, had not misjudged this one. She'd known from the start he was out of her league. Ariana Fitzpatrick, pregnant, guilt-ridden, and totally screwed-up, had no business messing with Mr. Perfect.

She loved this man, but he couldn't help it if he didn't love her in return. No point in leaving a good and decent man with a load of unearned guilt.

Drawing in a fortifying breath, the white lie slid off her tongue. The taste was acid.

"I think you may have been right."

"About what?" His tone was gentle, concerned.

"Hormones." She waved her hand airily. "Seeing the babies, feeling all that intense emotion in your presence got to me. That's all. I really didn't mean..." She couldn't bring herself to deny something as beautiful and sacred as love. Her voice trailed off. "Anything."

"No?" Eyes narrowing, he stared at her, appearing much less relieved than she'd expected. His next words told her why. "I don't believe you."

"Why, Mr. Lawson, how conceited of you."

He laughed, a self-deprecating sound. "You've got me there."

Ariana studied the blustery autumn day outside the car's warm interior, feeling as battered as the wind-whipped leaves. Soul weary and heart broken, she knew what she had to do.

"We've spent far too much time together; that's the problem. Under the circumstances I think we shouldn't see each other for a while. Then these troublesome hormones will disappear and everything will return to normal." In truth, she'd forgotten what normal was. She couldn't imagine a day without Grant, without his silly jokes or rock-steady presence.

"Not see each other?" Frowning, he pinched his bottom lip, his expression disturbed. "But I promised to be with you until the twins arrive. You need me."

"Grant, I thank you for all you've done, but the twins will arrive soon, safe and sound." Grappling for the door handle, she exited the car quickly before he could play knight-in-shining-armor and see her into the building. And before she self-destructed on his fancy leather car seat. "I no longer require your assistance."

"All right, then." Tone going flat, his solemn gaze measured her. "If that's what you want. But I am not leaving you completely alone. If you don't want me around, I'll hire someone else to look in on you."

Not want him around? He was the one rejecting her. Didn't he understand how shattered she would be to see him day after day knowing they had no future? "That won't be necessary. I've been taking care of myself for a long time."

The blue gaze turned to ice. "I insist."

His behavior puzzled her, but she was too upset to question it. She had to escape, to get away before she made a complete fool of herself by breaking down.

"Whatever makes you happy. Goodbye, Grant." Putting on her best imitation of a smile, she slammed the car door.

Hurrying up the walk, the sky as overcast as her mood, Ariana felt his eyes on her, but she refused to look back. For a little while she'd lived in a fantasy, hoping Grant would fall in love with her as she had with him. Every day spent with him had increased the hope, but now all hope was dashed.

For once, she'd made the proper decision. She'd released him, set him free from his overactive sense of chivalry.

Hand on the rail to pull her pregnant body up the stairs, she thought back over the weeks with Grant— to his steadfast loyalty and decency. To his humor and generosity. Fully, deeply entrenched in her heart and life, Grant was a man she couldn't forget.

Inside the cozy apartment, her inner storm broke loose. She leaned against the door as a tidal wave of anguish flooded her.

A tear slipped down her cheek. Then another.

Why hadn't she kept her feelings to herself? Why had she blurted out her love and destroyed their beautiful friendship?

Everywhere she looked, reminders of Grant tormented her. Two sterling silver piggybanks he'd bought today still rested in boxes on the coffee table. She visualized him in the kitchen, dish towel around his waist. At the table playing checkers with Roger. In the bedroom smoothing teddy bear boarder above the cribs.

"Oh, Grant. I love you so much."

Stumbling into the bedroom, she went to one crib, wound the mobile and let Brahm's lullaby fill the room. Grant chose this, just as he'd chosen all the babies' items, with exquisite care. He'd put so much love into this room. Why hadn't she understood this was all the love he had to offer?

Sobs broke free, tearing at her chest and throat. Like a fool, she stroked her hands over the crib rails as if his touch still warmed the smooth wood. Tears dotted the red and blue comforter.

Was it only last night that he'd kissed her? And she'd begun to believe, in spite of his statement to the contrary, that he might love her, too?

When she could stand the grief no longer, she lay down on the bed, curled onto her side and longed for sleep. Her back ached terribly, but her heart ached more. Visions of Grant as he saw the babies for the first time, tumbled together with the emptiness in his face when he'd driven away.

The mobile ran down, the lullaby ceased and silence descended.

She was drifting toward the edge of exhausted slumber when a knock sounded, jolting her upright.

"Grant," she whispered, hoping.

Rolling to a stand, much faster than she'd thought possible considering the pain in her back, she hurried to the door and yanked it open.

Hope tumbled to her toenails.

"Benjy."

He pushed his way past her, entering the apartment as if he had every right to be there.

"Where have you been? I came by earlier."

"Not that my whereabouts are any of your business, but I had a doctor's appointment. I'm pregnant, you know."

"Yeah, I heard. Loud and clear." His gaze shifted to her midsection, then slid away as if he found the sight distasteful. "Look, Ariana, I can't afford to pay child support. You know that. Come on, give me a break."

She hadn't seen him since the day he'd walked out, and now he waltzed into her apartment making demands, without a word of concern for her or his unborn children.

"The twins and I are doing well, all things considered. Thank you for asking." She gestured toward the open door. "Now, if you don't mind. I'd like you to leave."

The arrogance leaked out of him like air from a punctured tire. "Come on, babe," he whined, trying to touch her. "Don't be mad. We can work this out."

Skin crawling at the thought of his hands on her, Ariana sidestepped him. "There is nothing left to work out, Benjy, other than a child support agreement and the repayment of my life savings. You made your intentions very clear the day you left me waiting at the courthouse for hours while you moved in with your latest girlfriend.''

Benjy pushed the door shut, then backed against the white wood. Tilting his head to one side, he tried his sad puppy look. ''Is that what's bothering you, sugar? You're jealous? Why don't you drop this silly court case, and maybe you and me can get back together again?''

He thought she was jealous? What had she ever seen in this guy?

For months she'd planned this moment, wanting to tell Benjy exactly what she thought of his heartless abandonment. But now, as she looked into his weak, conniving face and found him woefully lacking in manhood, Ariana only wanted him gone from her life forever.

Anger eased up the back of her neck, setting her hair on end. ''Let me get this straight. You're willing to resume our engagement and get married in exchange for me dropping the lawsuit and forgetting about the sizeable amount of money you *borrowed* from me.''

''I thought you'd listen to reason, once you got past being mad at me.'' He moved forward, wearing a lopsided smile; a tactic he used, Ariana knew, to get his way. She was embarrassed to remember the number of times that that look had worked on her.

Staring at the face she'd once considered charming, Ariana now saw a weak and grabby Peter Pan who refused to grow up. Before, she would have run to his aid, feeling sorry for him, trying to fix his problems. Today she saw him for what he was, a user.

Grant's strong honorable image filled her mind.

Knowing him had opened her eyes to what a real man should be.

"Benjy, you and I were wrong for each other from the beginning. I wish I'd been wise enough to see that then and saved us both a lot of grief, but I didn't. I thought I could make you happy. Instead we made each other miserable."

The engaging grin fell away. His blue eyes, so different from Grant's, narrowed. "All this is your fault, you know. I never wanted to be saddled with kids. You did that, not me, and I don't intend to pay for your mistake. So, you might as well save the legal fees. You're not getting a dime from me—now or ever."

"You'll have to take that up with my attorney."

The mere mention of Grant stabbed at her with a thousand pinpricks. Would he continue to represent her now that she'd broken off personal contact?

"Your attorney?" Benjy jerked. "You mean Lawson?"

Benjy's reaction puzzled her. "Yes. Grant Lawson, my lawyer."

Lips twisted into a sneer, he raked her with is eyes. "Are you sure that's all he is?"

Ariana stiffened, itching to slap the sneer off his face. "Exactly what do you mean by that?"

"I went to see him today, to talk man-to-man, to make him understand my dilemma."

Ariana stifled a smile. The immature Benjy talking man-to-man with Grant? Get real. "And did Grant come around to your way of thinking?"

"The man is a maniac." He touched his lip. For the first time, Ariana noticed a slight swelling there. "Attacked me for no good reason."

"Attacked? You mean to tell me that Grant Lawson hit you?" Unbelievable. "Why?"

"That's what I'm asking you. Why is your lawyer getting so worked up over a disagreement between a man and his fiancée?"

"Ex-fiancée," she said automatically, unable to get over this latest revelation. Sensible, cool, controlled Grant had punched Benjy's pouty face? "Grant really hit you?"

"You and him got something going, don't you?"

Her feelings for Grant were far too wonderful to discuss with Benjy. "You can leave now. Our conversation is over."

Pressing a hand to the small of her back, she reached around him to open the door. He grabbed her arm. "I got news for you, Ariana. No matter what any blood test says, I will never believe those kids are mine. For all I know they belong to that fancy lawyer."

At that moment, Ariana understood the saying that it takes more than biology to make a man a father, and Benjy would never be a father to her children.

Glaring down at his grip, she said, "You know what, Benjy? Maybe they're not yours."

Mouth going slack with shock, he released her and fell back. "You're admitting it?"

"I'll make a deal with you. You relinquish all rights to the twins and I'll drop the support claim permanently. You can even forget about the money you owe me."

"That's it?" He looked as though he'd won the grand prize on a game show. "That's all I have to do and you'll get off my back?"

"That's all you have to do," she answered with a sad smile. "I can have my attorney draw up the papers, we sign them and we'll be out of each other's lives forever."

An annoyingly pleased grin appeared. "I knew you

weren't the kind of woman to punish a man forever for one little mistake.'' This time he opened the door himself. A draft of cool air swirled up the hallway. ''Get those papers drawn up and I'll be happy to sign on the dotted line.''

A little piece of her splintered. The fool had no idea what he was giving up, and furthermore he didn't care. For Benjy, the twins would always be a ''little mistake.''

''I'll do that.'' Ariana waited for him to leave, watched him step jauntily down the hall, as blemished a person now as he had been when they'd first met. But Benjamin Walburn was no longer her problem to fix.

Astonished at how well she'd handled the situation, a sense of pride shot through her. Somewhere between preparing to be a mother and falling in love with a real man, she'd learned a few things. Change came from within. Regardless of her encouragement, Benjy hadn't grown because he chose not to. She, on the other hand, had changed a great deal.

Grant, that wonderful, bossy man, had given her more than baby furniture.

She was a better person for loving such a fine human being. Wiser. Stronger. *More.*

He was worth every bit of the love aching in her chest, and she would never regret their time together.

She had been a coward before, but no more.

Heading straight to the telephone, she picked up the receiver and dialed the memorized number in Florida.

''Hello, Mama?'' Her voice filled with resolve. ''It's me, Ariana. I have something very important to tell you…''

Chapter Eleven

Grant kept hearing her warm, husky voice proclaiming love and wishing he was the father of her children. Heaven knew he cared for her, and he cared for the twins, but love? Marriage? He couldn't go through that again. Regardless of the impact Ariana had had on his life, he'd settled that issue a long time ago. Or perhaps Tiffany had settled it for him with her cold taunts of his inadequacy, his ineffectiveness as a man, as a husband. Whichever, he'd come to the conclusion that he did not have what it took to be a husband or a father.

Pacing the pristine-white tile of his kitchen, his life felt as sterile and void as this condo Tiffany had decorated.

He poured a cup of coffee and sipped, grimacing when the hot brew singed his tongue.

His sleep last night had been fraught with dreams of Ariana running toward him on the beach, laughing her musical laugh. Two munchkins with her changeable eyes reached out to him, and his heart had soared with happiness. Futile, senseless, impossible dreams.

Today was Saturday, but he considered going into work just the same. Anything to get his mind off Ariana—something an hour and a half at the gym hadn't accomplished.

Carrying the cup to the table, he flipped open his laptop, but his attention strayed to the bright centerpiece on the glass-topped table. Ariana had placed the red silk flowers there, adding color to his apartment just as she'd brought light and color into every facet of his world.

He reached out, stroking the soft petals between his finger and thumb, petals almost as soft as Ariana's skin.

She'd tried to take back her words of love, and for those few bewildering moments he'd believed her. But as he'd watched her walk away, defeat in every step, he realized she'd told another of her white lies to spare him.

His chest expanded, and he listened to his own breath rush out, the only sound in his lonely apartment.

The logical, rational lawyer in him knew she'd made the right decision, breaking things off this way. Considering her feelings, any further time together would only complicate matters more. But the man in him howled in protest at losing her. He hadn't been ready for that. Not yet. Soon, he knew, but not quite yet.

Tapping the computer keys, he called up his e-mail, deleting junk mail and scrolling past business messages to read the personal posts. One from Vanessa caught his eye. He smiled, glad to hear from the sister who could lift his mood on the worst of days.

And he had to admit today was one of the worst. He took a sip of sweetened coffee and read:

*Hi, Big Bro, Dad tells me you turned down his offer.
Good going, you brave man. Here are some photos I
snapped at the beach house. If you don't see what I
see in these, you need laser surgery. Enjoy!*

Puzzled, Grant clicked on the attachment and waited
as inch by inch, Vanessa's magical art appeared. The
first one knocked the air out of him.

The cup thunked against the table, sloshing coffee
on the fastidiously polished glass. He left it. Collapsing
into a chair, he could only stare, frozen, paralyzed by
the powerful picture splashed across his computer
screen.

Silhouetted against a backdrop of moon and sea, he
and Ariana stood in an embrace, so tender it made
Grant's chest ache. Though her abdomen rounded into
his, their noses touched, and his mouth hovered a whisper from hers. Two lovers, their unborn child between
them, kissing on the beach. A photo so charged with
emotion as to create a physical hunger in him to hold
Ariana once more.

When and how had Vanessa snapped this without
alerting either Ariana or him? Vanessa, the artistic eye
that never missed an undercurrent, had seen what he
hadn't. Her stuffy, unemotional brother was falling in
love.

With a ragged sigh, he fell back in the chair. Heaven
help him. He loved Ariana Fitzpatrick. And she
claimed to love him, too.

A kind of wild hope flared in him, then quickly died.
They had come together during a crisis point in her life
and she had clung to him as a safe harbor in a storm.
What she felt was not love, but need spurred on by
pregnancy hormones. Once the twins arrived and her
life was back in order, she wouldn't need him at all.

And that was fine. That was best. Ariana deserved to be loved totally and completely. He would never be enough.

Touching his index finger to his lips, Grant then lay the tip against the screen, holding it there while his coffee grew cold and his resolve grew stronger. He'd made the right decision and so had she.

Ariana disembarked the city bus and stepped upon the curb, holding a picnic basket with one hand and her back with the other. Behind her the bus belched exhaust, then roared away into the cold sunlight of a perfect autumn day.

She'd tossed and turned most of last night, overjoyed at the conversation with her mother, relieved to have solved the situation with Benjy once and for all, and devastated to have so misjudged the relationship with Grant. Finally at the crack of dawn, the nagging back-ache had become an incessant pressure that no position would relieve, so she'd risen to bake a casserole—always a therapeutic action—and to make some plans.

For months now she'd floundered, letting life's wind blow her wherever it would, but somewhere in the night she'd come to a decision to take charge of her life.

Climbing the three steps to Grant's condo was harder than she'd ever anticipated, and she was panting for breath by the time he yanked the door open and scowled at her.

"What are you doing here?" His face was a thunderhead.

Ariana fell back, hurt. She'd never considered that he might not want to see her at all, ever.

"I'm sorry. I had something important to tell you, but I can leave if you like."

He jerked the basket from her hand. "Get in here and sit down."

He pulled her inside the apartment and guided her to a chair. "You're supposed to be home in bed."

The light dawned. "Is that what you're so upset about?"

"Of course. Why else?" He frowned at her.

Ariana smiled and shook her head. "Never mind."

Setting the basket on the floor, he sat on the couch next to her chair, realization narrowing his blue, blue eyes. "You thought I didn't want you here. Is that it?"

"Right again, counselor."

"Don't be ridiculous." He shoved an ottoman toward her. "Put your feet up."

"Bossy, bossy, bossy." With a sigh, she did exactly as she was told, pleased that he cared. The ache in her back didn't improve one iota.

Hands on his knees, Grant leaned forward. "Now what was so important that you disobeyed doctors orders and came over here?"

"First of all, I wanted to thank you for all you've done."

"You could have done that over the telephone."

She knew he was right, as always, but she'd convinced herself that she needed to see him again when she wasn't so distressed. But in truth, she'd wanted to see his beloved face one more time before they became nothing but casual acquaintances again, working in the same company.

"There are other reasons, too." She arched her back, searching for a comfortable position. "I called Mama last night. She's coming to Boston as soon as she can make arrangements with my sister to look after Aunt Lily for a while.''

"How did she take the news?''

"I'd misjudged her, Grant.'' Regret pulled at Ariana over the time she'd wasted. "Mama wasn't disappointed in me at all, only sad that I felt I had to hide the truth from the people who love me the most.''

Expression smug, Grant didn't say I told you so. Instead he said, "I'm glad, angel. You need your family now.''

Yes, she needed them now more than ever. Now that Grant no longer wanted to be a part of her life.

"So you can stop worrying about me. I am going to be fine. In fact, Mama wants me to move back to Florida.''

Grant gave her a long, cold stare. "And are you?''

Ariana lifted one shoulder. "I'm considering it. Having family around would be good for the twins.''

When Mama first broached the subject, Ariana had outright rejected the notion. Move? So far away from Grant? Away from Boston and the job she enjoyed? But after serious thought, maybe getting away from Boston and memories of a love she couldn't have would be the best for both of them.

"I see.'' Grant's face closed up. Pinching his top lip, he stared into space. "So, when are you leaving?''

"Oh, I don't know. I haven't made up my mind yet, but certainly not until after the babies arrive and the papers with Benjy are signed.''

Grant afforded her a glance, saw her arch her back again, and brought her a throw pillow. "What papers?''

She leaned forward, allowing him to slide the pillow behind her back. His wonderful smell wafted around her and she almost lost her chipper resolve to show him the mature, together woman she really was.

"That's my other news. I won't need your legal help anymore, either. Once the papers are signed, I mean."

"Explain."

"Benjy came by last night."

"What did he want?" Grant looked absolutely feral.

"To weasel out of supporting the twins."

"Figures."

"I let him."

He sat bolt upright. "You did what?"

"Benjy, the creep, does not believe the twins are his. Made some crude remarks about my fidelity—" Noting the angry flush on Grant's face, she suddenly understood why he had punched Benjy yesterday. "But you already knew that, didn't you?"

"Mr. Walburn was a busy man yesterday. He also paid a visit to my office. I didn't want you to know the unkind things he said."

His admission warmed her. "Benjy has no power to hurt me anymore, Grant. I never loved him. I tried to because he needed me so badly—or so I thought." She smiled ruefully. "But I never really loved him. Now that he's eagerly agreed to give up all rights to the babies in exchange for my agreement never to ask for support, I am relieved to have him out of my life forever."

Suddenly she felt really strange. A wave of inexplicable heat washed through her body. Sweat popped out on her forehead and her pulse pounded in her throat as though she'd drunk too much coffee.

Scooting to the edge of the chair, she stood. "I need to go now, Grant."

With his athletic grace, he shot up and motioned hopefully toward the basket. "We have a casserole."

She shook her head. "Sorry. You're on your own. I need to lie down. My back is killing me and I feel sort of funny."

Alarmed, Grant took her arm. "I'll drive you home."

"Okay. Maybe you should." She got as far as the door before something warm and wet gushed from her body. "Oh, no, your white carpet."

Grant's eyes went wide. "Carpet be hanged. You're in labor."

"Can't be." She stroked her belly. "My back hurts like crazy, but I haven't had a single contraction." As soon as she said the words she remembered. "Back labor. I read about that but didn't know what it was."

"Back labor?" His voice rose in terror. "How long has this been going on?"

"All night. But the discomfort is worse this morning. A lot worse." She bent forward trying to relieve the pressure.

"Let's get you to the hospital."

He disappeared and returned almost immediately with his car keys. By this time, Ariana hung on to the wall, panting. "I can't move."

"I'll carry you." He reached for her.

"Don't touch me." He jerked back. She grabbed for the wall and moaned. "Grant, the babies are coming."

"They can't. We're not at the hospital."

"Amelia doesn't know that." The pain in her back became a violent pressure, tearing downward. "Oh, shoot. Oh, Grant. I have to lie down."

"Pant, breathe, chant. Whatever it is they tell you to do. I'm calling 911."

Ariana fought a hysterical giggle. Calm, collected Grant was rattled.

When another moan overtook her, Grant swept her into his arms and headed for the bedroom where he gently lay her on the whitest satin comforter she'd ever seen.

"I'll ruin your comforter."

"I'm looking for an excuse to redecorate. Now, hush."

He grabbed for the phone and punched in the numbers. Meanwhile, Ariana concentrated on remembering everything she'd learned in birthing classes.

"Great, just great," Grant murmured, then slammed the phone into its cradle and turned to her. "There's a huge pile-up on the interstate. We may have a while before an ambulance arrives."

Ariana grabbed for his hand as a killer contraction took control. Sweat popped out all over her. "We won't make it. The babies are coming *now.*"

Pain clenched her back, ripping her in two. She moaned, bearing down on Grant's hand in desperation.

"I wanted to be brave," she cried, calm and reason fleeing. "But I'm scared. Really scared."

"Angel, you're the bravest person I know." As if gaining strength from her sudden display of weakness, Grant took over, calm and confidence returning. "Now take a deep breath and concentrate on all the things we've learned. We're a team, you and me. We're going to be fine."

Focusing on his beloved voice, she followed his instructions, thankful for the childbirth video they'd watched together countless times. Letting her body's natural demands lead them, she sweated and groaned, pushed and prayed.

From somewhere in the fog of pain and confusion, she heard a voice say, "I love you, angel. You can do this. I love you."

She longed to answer, to make sense of the words, but the demands of birth proved too great.

Then, in a sudden rush, the agony disappeared. A lusty wail of protest filled the room.

"Amelia Rose. A beauty," Grant said reverently. "Like her mama."

Full of love and wonder, Ariana wanted to shout for joy. But before she had time to enjoy the moment the vicious cycle started again.

Her eyes glazed over and Grant knew immediately what was happening. His pulse kicked into high gear. The second baby. The one that might be turned in the wrong direction. Heaven help him. What would he do if something happened to Ariana or her son?

In the distance a siren wailed, but this baby wasn't waiting for the ambulance to arrive.

A torrent of anxiety set Grant's hands to trembling. Through sheer force of will he calmed them. Ariana needed him and he would not let her down. Not again. Not like he had yesterday.

Sweat beaded his forehead. He loved this woman. He loved these children. They were his in every way that counted, and nothing—*nothing*—was going to happen to them as long as he had life in his body.

The realization stunned him to the marrow. He couldn't let Ariana go off to Florida and take the babies—*his* babies. He loved them too much and had for a long time though he'd been in such denial, such fear that he hadn't seen what his wise sister had.

Suddenly he knew how wrong he'd been. How

wrong Tiffany had been. He wasn't a cold, unfeeling clod.

Right now, his chest hurt so much with love for Ariana, he thought he would burst. And the terror he felt was white hot. If he lost her—

"Grant!" Ariana's cry shocked him into action. Looking into her glazed, pain filled eyes, he was willing to take on the world in her behalf. This delicate angel had taught him what real love, real emotion was all about. A pure heart, she would never betray him.

"I love you, angel. Everything is going to be fine." He prayed he was right. "We're almost there."

As though his words strengthened her she nodded once, then curled forward, her gaze locked on his. Face flushed and soaked with sweat she was the most beautiful woman he'd ever seen.

Though the agony seemed to go on forever another cry soon joined the first one as little Christopher made his grand entrance.

A third sound intruded as the paramedics arrived. Grant hurried to let them in and they took over. He stood back, relieved but watchful. This was *his* family. He had so much inside him, so much he needed to tell Ariana, but he'd waited a lifetime to feel this way. First, he'd make sure she was okay. And then he'd show her his heart.

Ariana was asleep when Grant finally received permission to take the twins into her hospital room. She lay like a dark angel among the snowy sheets at Massachusetts General while he, the unemotional lawyer stood beside her bed, cradling a baby in each arm, tears in his eyes.

"Hey, beautiful," he said softly, not at all surprised at the tremble in his voice.

She opened tired eyes, her pale lips lifting in a mother's smile. "My babies. Are they okay?"

No thought of herself or what she'd been through; all her focus was on her babies. Moved, awed, amazed at this fragile, valiant woman, Grant could no longer envision a life without her.

"They're perfect." The mattress tilted as he leaned down to snuggle the babies against her side and kiss her forehead. "You're perfect."

Her smile widened to include him. "You're pretty awesome yourself, Doctor Lawson. If I had to have the twins today, I'm glad you were with us. I needed you. I…"

She stopped short, but Grant heard the hesitancy and suspected what she wanted to say, but couldn't. Because he'd been such a fool.

He dropped to his knees beside the bed and took her hand.

"Do you still love me, Ariana?"

A puzzled expression crossed her features, but Ariana lifted her chin slightly and admitted, "Yes, I do. Whether you want me or not makes no difference."

His heart shattered. He'd hurt her so much and yet, she still boldly asserted her love for him. "I want you."

"But yesterday—"

"Forget yesterday. Yesterday I was a scared, irrational idiot who thought I didn't have what it took to love anyone, but I was wrong. I love you, Ariana. And I love these babies." He stroked a finger over Christopher's downy head. "I can't promise you a lifetime of parties—"

"I don't want parties."

"Hush. I'm trying to say something important here."

"Bossy." But she hushed, drawing the twins closer to her side, her gaze never leaving his face.

"I know I'm not Mr. Excitement. I'm a stay at home kind of guy who probably thinks too much and works more than I should. But if you'll marry me, I'll give you everything I have and all that I am for the rest of my life. I love you, Ariana."

A radiant smile lit her face. "You're the most exciting, amazing man I've ever met. And I love you, too. Nothing would make me happier or prouder than to be your wife. Now, will you please kiss me? I've had a rough day."

Flooded with love for this woman who'd filled the vast, empty chasm inside him, Grant laughed with unbridled joy...then did as she asked.

Epilogue

The conference room of Wintersoft, Inc. buzzed with energy and several dozen friends and co-workers. Today was the twins' first official outing—in the form of a company baby shower. To Ariana's delight even the men, including CEO Lloyd Winters, had taken a few minutes out of the day to drink sparkling punch, eat cake and admire Christopher and Amelia. Ariana was sure she could credit Grant for that accomplishment.

Standing beside her, resplendent in a dark suit and red tie, he leaned toward her. Her breath, filled with his wonderful sandalwood scent, caught in her throat.

Ariana still could hardly believe that Grant had feared falling in love. That he'd doubted his own ability to be a proper husband and father. And she thanked God every day for the unorthodox birth of her children—she smiled—their children, since Grant fully intended to adopt them as soon as they were married.

"I don't think your mama plans to relinquish those babies for a second."

Ariana smiled toward her mother, overjoyed to have her in Boston. Indeed, Mama had hardly let the twins out of her sight since her arrival last week. Even now, in a room full of well-wishers who were dying to get their hands on the babies, her mother held a twin in each arm and swayed from side to side crooning a soft Spanish lullaby. A strong man couldn't muscle them out of her arms. "She's in love."

Heat flared in Grant's blue eyes. "So am I. And I'm ready to tell the whole world."

Taking her hand, he moved through the crowd to the long table where gaily colored gifts and bright congratulatory balloons waited. They'd agreed to make their official announcement today while everyone was gathered together. Excitement danced along her nerve endings.

"May I have your attention?" Grant called, raising his voice. A chorus of *shhs* went up around the room as all eyes turned to them.

When the crowd quieted, he fumbled in his jacket, pulling out a ring box. A gasp lodged in Ariana's throat. He hadn't told her about this.

"Ariana and I thank all of you for coming to celebrate the new additions, and as exciting as they are, we have some more exciting news to share." Eyes never leaving her face, he clicked open the box. Ariana's mouth fell open. "I am both delighted and honored to announce that Ariana has agreed to be my wife." He slipped a glittering solitaire onto her finger. "But in all this business of having babies and getting settled, she's yet to tell me exactly how long I'll have to wait." He lifted an eyebrow. "Ariana?"

Blissfully happy, one hand pressed to her joyful heart, Ariana replied, "How about—" she grappled for an appropriate time frame, knowing Grant was as anxious as she ''—two months from now.''

''The sooner the better,'' he growled and swooped in to seal the moment with a kiss. Laughter and applause filled the room.

Brett Hamilton, their handsome British co-worker rose and came toward them, clinking an ink pen on the side of his punch glass.

When the hubbub finally ceased, he said, ''I do believe a toast is in order.'' He raised his glass. ''To the happy couple.''

Cries of ''Hear! Hear!'' went up around the room.

Standing to the side, Emily Winters clinked her glass against Carmella's, pleased that Ariana and Grant had fallen in love, and relieved that bachelor number two was on his way to the altar with little or no help from Carmella and her. Her glance fell to the toast-maker, Brett Hamilton. Bachelor number three, on the other hand, could present a greater challenge. Only a few minutes before this party began Carmella had rushed into Emily's office with a shocking revelation.

''Emily, look.'' Breathless, Carmella had waved a paper. ''You are not going to believe this, but Brett Hamilton is part of *the* Hamilton family of Great Britain. I found this on the Internet.''

She shoved a royal wedding picture beneath Emily's nose. And there he was big as life and every bit as handsome—their very own co-worker, Brett Hamilton.

Emily had gasped in surprise. Even now her head reeled from the news. Breton Hamilton was more than Wintersoft's vice president of Overseas Operations. He was a member of royalty, a bona fide British lord. With that kind of background and his good looks, finding

Brett a "princess" and guiding him to a fairy-tale wedding should be no trouble at all.

Someone snapped a picture and Ariana, still wrapped in Grant's arms, pulled back to find the source. Vanessa, her future sister-in-law, waved from three feet away. Beside her, wearing pleased smiles were the rest of the Lawson family.

"Grant said he had something special in mind today." With a grin, Vanessa wiggled her camera. "Couldn't miss the photo-op."

Grant's parents wove through the crowd toward the newly engaged couple. To Ariana's surprised delight Suzanne reached her first and pulled her into an embrace.

"Thank you, my dear." Mrs. Lawson stepped back, smiling, her elegant perfume warming the space in between.

Ariana shot Grant a puzzled glance. He winked and looped an arm around her waist. "You're welcome, of course, but I'm not sure why you're thanking me."

"For putting the joy back into my son's life. All I ever wanted was to see him as fulfilled as he is today."

"He's done the same for me, Mrs. Lawson. And I will do everything within my power to keep him happy from now on."

"I know that, dear, or I wouldn't be here offering my blessings." She gave Ariana's arm a pat. "And it's Suzanne, please. You're family now."

Vanessa snapped another picture as the two women embraced once again.

The flash awakened baby Christopher who began to fuss. Ariana started to him, but Mama waved her away, beaming a radiant smile. "No, no, *caro*. Suzanne and I will take care of him."

"Come back here, angel," Grant said, tugging on her hand. "Vanessa needs more pictures. Wouldn't want to miss the photo-op." He pumped his eyebrows wickedly, then pulled her into his arms again and kissed her senseless while their beaming families looked on and the camera flashed.

When the glorious moment ended, bemused and blissful, Ariana rested her thoroughly kissed and blushing face against Grant's strong, muscled chest. Beneath the rough wool of his suit, Ariana listened to the steady thump of Grant's heart, knowing that he loved her with every beat. All doubts were gone now. And she loved him with a devotion as true as the sun and every bit as bright.

"I love you, angel," she heard him say, and joy bloomed in her like a fragrant rose.

For Ariana and Grant the world had finally righted itself. Life was good. Very, very good.

And the future promised to be even better.

* * * * *

Turn the page for a sneak preview of the next
MARRYING THE BOSS'S DAUGHTER *title*
featuring Brett and Sunny's hilarious,
heart-warming story: FILL-IN FIANCÉE
by DeAnna Talcott
on sale November 2003 (SR1694)

And don't miss any of the books in the
MARRYING THE BOSS'S DAUGHTER *series*
only available from Silhouette Romance:

Chapter One

"What with their upcoming visit, I'd imagine Mother and Father will take the opportunity to remind you of your duties and obligations."

Brett's eyes shuttered closed, and he was grateful his brother on the other end of the line couldn't witness his exasperation. His parents had been nagging him for years to settle down and get married. "So you're warning me?"

"Well?" Phillip prodded. "What about your love life? You've been suspiciously quiet about it since you've moved to the other side of the ocean. It's made Mother think that maybe you've had regrets, and with Lady Harriet, perhaps that absence has made the heart grow fonder. She even mentioned that Lady Harriet might consider joining them on their visit to Boston. She hinted to Mother that she's never been there."

The suggestion brought Brett out of his reverie, and his shoulders lifted off the leather desk chair. "What?"

A second slipped away as he tried to reconstruct Phillip's intent. "No. Absolutely not."

"Why not?"

"Well for one thing, I'll not be forced into a marriage and for another, we're simply not compatible. We established that two years ago."

"You grow to like your mate, Brett."

Mate? Damn, he loathed the functional term. The woman he'd spend the rest of his life with would meet his expectations on every level, including the emotional and the spiritual. The last thing he needed was Lady Harriet to tag along on his parent's visit. "But I've grown to like my girlfriend," he said coyly, thinking that if he said he already had a woman in his life, they'd drop the whole thing. "Here. In Boston."

"Say again?" Brett heard two sharp raps, most likely against the receiver. "I do say there must be something wrong with the connection. You? Have a girlfriend?"

"More than that," Brett went on boldly. "We're engaged."

A moment of dead silence followed his declaration.

"I beg your pardon, man? And you've been keeping it quiet! What a cagey old bloke, you are!"

"I'm not trying to be cagey." But Brett's enthusiasm for the broad picture he'd painted grew. If his brother believed the tale, maybe he could get off the hook with his parents as well. He'd had quite enough of their hints—and their ultimatums. "And there's more," he claimed, baiting his brother with one last delectable tidbit that had soared through his imagination. "We're living together."

"What! And you've stayed mum about all this?"

"I wasn't quite prepared to tell everyone. Not yet."

"You realize you have just poked a hole in Mother and Father's carefully laid plans?"

"Mmm. Maybe. But you can see that if Lady Harriet chose to surprise me with a visit—well, it would be most…uncomfortable."

As he was ruminating his way around this particularly tricky scenario, Sunny Robbins rapped on the frame of his open door. Seeing he was on the phone, she politely held up a file folder of contracts he'd requested an hour ago. He motioned for her to come in.

Sunny, who had the most mesmerizing gait of any woman who walked through Wintersoft's legal department, crossed the threshold and entered his domain. She was wearing that same short skirt again. The one he'd noticed her in in the employee's lounge last week. Huh. Short enough to play with a man's imagination, long enough to be respectable.

She had coltish legs, and they matched her demeanor—a little unconventional, and very unencumbered. He'd always wondered about her, and had recently struck up several conversations with her that stopped just short of him asking her out. She was the paralegal who worked for Grant Lawson, General Counsel for the company.

"I've got the copies," she whispered, preparing to put them on his desk.

"Wait," he mouthed, lifting a finger, and listening to his brother's tirade.

She slid them on the corner of his desk and took a step back.

"I don't believe it! Someone has snared my little brother? The man who always said it would take one resourceful temptress to steal his bachelorhood? That was the most inviting thing about you and the girls, you know. You were unattainable.''

At that precise moment, Sunny threaded her fingers through her tawny streaked hair and raked the chin-length riot of blunt cut, windswept hair back from her temple. Her smile, patient and unaffected, as she waited for him to get off the phone, accelerated his heartbeat. Their gazes collided and in that brief pause he saw something in Sunny Robbins that he'd never before recognized—and it was a vision that coincided with the remark Phillip made about his "resourceful temptress."

"Yes, well, I'm one step closer to giving it up," Brett confirmed, determined to stay fastened to the charade but equally uneasy about the direction his wild ploy was taking him.

"Who *is* this woman?" his brother pressed. "What does she do? Where is she?"

"Actually, she's right here," Brett declared recklessly. "Sunny," he summoned, "blow my brother a kiss, will you, luv?"

Sunny blinked, and then her eyebrows furrowed. "Excuse me?"

"Blow him a kiss. From your lovely lips to my only brother, a half a world away."

"Why?" Sunny slanted him a dubious look.

Brett grew magnanimous, like he always did when he carried a plot too far. This one was going to get him in big trouble, he knew it. He could just feel it. "Because he wants to meet you! Tell my brother I love my job, I love my life. Blow him a kiss, and assure him all is well with the world. That all is well with you." He handed Sunny the phone.

She stared at it, as if he'd taken complete leave of his senses. When she finally, reluctantly, accepted it, she put it to her ear and listened, as if she expected to hear something absurd.

Then, to Brett's delight, she made a sloppy smacking noise into the receiver.

"Yes, I'm fine," she said tentatively.

Brett's smile grew, and his confidence multiplied. He couldn't help it, he looked at the conference call button and popped it on.

"And I hear you're engaged to my brother."

"I'm what!" Sunny exclaimed....

Your opinion is important to us! Please take a few moments to share your thoughts with us about your experiences with Harlequin and Silhouette books. Your comments will be very useful in ensuring that we deliver books you love to read.
Please take a few minutes to complete the questionnaire, then send it to us at the address below.

Send your completed questionnaires to:
Harlequin/Silhouette Reader Survey, P.O. Box 9046, Buffalo, NY 14269-9046

1. As you may know, there are many different lines under the Harlequin and Silhouette brands. Each of the lines is listed below. Please check the box that most represents your reading habit for each line.

Line	Currently read this line	Do not read this line	Not sure if I read this line
Harlequin American Romance	❑	❑	❑
Harlequin Duets	❑	❑	❑
Harlequin Romance	❑	❑	❑
Harlequin Historicals	❑	❑	❑
Harlequin Superromance	❑	❑	❑
Harlequin Intrigue	❑	❑	❑
Harlequin Presents	❑	❑	❑
Harlequin Temptation	❑	❑	❑
Harlequin Blaze	❑	❑	❑
Silhouette Special Edition	❑	❑	❑
Silhouette Romance	❑	❑	❑
Silhouette Intimate Moments	❑	❑	❑
Silhouette Desire	❑	❑	❑

2. Which of the following best describes why you bought *this book?* One answer only, please.

the picture on the cover	❑	the title	❑
the author	❑	the line is one I read often	❑
part of a miniseries	❑	saw an ad in another book	❑
saw an ad in a magazine/newsletter	❑	a friend told me about it	❑
I borrowed/was given this book	❑	other: _____	❑

3. Where did you buy *this book?* One answer only, please.

at Barnes & Noble	❑	at a grocery store	❑
at Waldenbooks	❑	at a drugstore	❑
at Borders	❑	on eHarlequin.com Web site	❑
at another bookstore	❑	from another Web site	❑
at Wal-Mart	❑	Harlequin/Silhouette Reader	❑
at Target	❑	Service/through the mail	
at Kmart	❑	used books from anywhere	❑
at another department store or mass merchandiser	❑	I borrowed/was given this book	❑

4. On average, how many Harlequin and Silhouette books do you buy at one time?

I buy _____ books at one time	❑
I rarely buy a book	❑

MRQ403SR-1A

5. How many times per month do you shop for any *Harlequin and/or Silhouette* books?
One answer only, please.

1 or more times a week	❑	a few times per year	❑
1 to 3 times per month	❑	less often than once a year	❑
1 to 2 times every 3 months	❑	never	❑

6. When you think of your ideal heroine, which *one* statement describes her the best?
One answer only, please.

She's a woman who is strong-willed	❑	She's a desirable woman	❑
She's a woman who is needed by others	❑	She's a powerful woman	❑
She's a woman who is taken care of	❑	She's a passionate woman	❑
She's an adventurous woman	❑	She's a sensitive woman	❑

7. The following statements describe types or genres of books that you may be
interested in reading. Pick *up to 2 types* of books that you are most interested in.

I like to read about truly romantic relationships	❑
I like to read stories that are sexy romances	❑
I like to read romantic comedies	❑
I like to read a romantic mystery/suspense	❑
I like to read about romantic adventures	❑
I like to read romance stories that involve family	❑
I like to read about a romance in times or places that I have never seen	❑
Other: _____	❑

*The following questions help us to group your answers with those readers who are
similar to you. Your answers will remain confidential.*

8. Please record your year of birth below.
19 _____

9. What is your marital status?
single ❑   married ❑   common-law ❑   widowed ❑
divorced/separated ❑

10. Do you have children 18 years of age or younger currently living at home?
yes ❑   no ❑

11. Which of the following best describes your employment status?
employed full-time or part-time ❑   homemaker ❑   student ❑
retired ❑   unemployed ❑

12. Do you have access to the Internet from either home or work?
yes ❑   no ❑

13. Have you ever visited eHarlequin.com?
yes ❑   no ❑

14. What state do you live in?
_____

15. Are you a member of Harlequin/Silhouette Reader Service?
yes ❑   Account # _____   no ❑   MRQ403SR-1B

SILHOUETTE *Romance*

COMING NEXT MONTH

#1694 FILL-IN FIANCÉE—DeAnna Talcott
Marrying the Boss's Daughter

Recruiting well-mannered beauty Sunny Robbins to pose as his bride-to-be was the perfect solution to Lord Breton Hamilton's biggest problem—his matchmaking parents! Sunny wasn't the titled English aristocrat they expected, but she was a more enticing alternative than *their* choices. And the way she sent his pulse racing… Was Brett's fill-in fiancée destined to become his lawfully—*lovingly*—wedded wife?

#1695 THE PRINCESS & THE MASKED MAN—
Valerie Parv
The Carramer Trust

Beautiful royals didn't propose marriages of convenience! Yet that's exactly what Princess Giselle de Marigny did when she discovered Bryce Laws's true identity. Since the widowed single father wanted a mother for his young daughter, he agreed to the plan. But Giselle's kisses stirred deeper feelings, and Bryce realized she might become keeper of his heart!

#1696 TO WED A SHEIK—Teresa Southwick
Desert Brides

Crown Prince Kamal Hassan promised never to succumb to the weakness of love, but Ali Matlock, his sexy new employee, was tempting him beyond all limits. The headstrong American had made it clear an office fling was out of the question. But for Kamal, so was giving up Ali. Would he trade his playboy lifestyle for a lifetime of happiness?

#1697 WEST TEXAS BRIDE—Madeline Baker
City girl Carly Kirkwood had about as much business on a Texas ranch as she did falling for rancher Zane Roan Eagle— none! Still, she couldn't deny her attraction to the handsome cowboy or the sparks that flew between them. Would she be able to leave the big city behind for Zane? And could she forgive him when the secrets of his past were revealed?

SRCNM1003